Boy Heroes
of Chapultepec

Boy Heroes
of Chapultepec

A Story of the Mexican War

By MARÍA CRISTINA CHAMBERS

Illustrated by Joseph Krush

WINSTON
ADVENTURE
BOOKS

CECILE MATSCHAT, *Editor*

CARL CARMER, *Consulting Editor*

THE JOHN C. WINSTON COMPANY
Philadelphia · Toronto

To

Gordon Fisk-Mullin

The Mexican War

SOME historians have claimed that the war of 1846–1848 with Mexico is a "foul blot upon our national honor." They contend that the war was fomented by slaveholders interested only in acquiring new territory. Actually, nothing could be further from the truth.

Texas had been an independent Republic for nine years before its annexation by the United States. Yet Mexico claimed this annexation as a cause for war. The United States sent an envoy to Mexico to discuss the disputed Texas boundary. Two successive Mexican presidents refused to receive him, afraid of the warlike spirit of the country.

President Polk, even after the beginning of the war, continued to negotiate for peace. His envoy, John Slidell of Louisiana, was unsuccessful, and Nicholas Trist was sent as a special peace envoy. Stationed with General Winfield Scott at Veracruz, his orders were to make peace with the dictator, Santa Anna, at the earliest possible moment.

In 1846 Santa Anna had been allowed to return to Mexico from exile in Cuba, because he had persuaded President Polk that he could negotiate a treaty of peace between Mexico and the United States. This premise was false. Yet when peace negotiations finally were achieved, Mexico was given almost as generous terms as before the Americans had stormed and won their capital. They received $15,000,000 in cash. The United States also agreed to pay the $3,500,000 that the Mexicans in 1840 had promised to pay American citizens, but later had repudiated. In return, Mexico ceded to the United States California and New Mexico, and agreed to recognize the Rio Grande as the southern and western boundary of Texas.

A few years ago, when President Harry Truman was on his way to a fiesta at the National Stadium in Mexico, he stopped at Chapultepec Park to lay a wreath on the monument to the six Mexican cadets who died in the defense of Chapultepec some one hundred years ago. This book is the story of that heroic defense, honored alike by Americans everywhere and their neighbors south of the border.

CECILE MATSCHAT, *Editor*
CARL CARMER, *Consulting Editor*

CONTENTS

CHAPTER 1

A Horseman at the Gate

PEDRO jumped from under the eucalyptus tree where he had taken refuge from the blazing sun with Pinto, and looked anxiously at the sky. The sun was still high over the distant hill and he wondered what time it was.

"Come, Pinto! It is time to close the gate."

He ran across the broad patio and the dog followed him to the great iron gate of the Manor House. As he ran, he looked to the right and left of the courtyard, hoping that Don Luis Ramos Blancos, his master, wasn't around. He could almost hear his loud, harsh voice commanding him, "I want the gate closed earlier."

"We must always close the gate before sunset,

1

and I almost forgot it." Pedro spoke to Pinto as if the dog were a person. "I wonder why!" he mumbled, while he pulled the heavy chains and padlocked the gate carefully.

The closing of the gate was now the most important of Pedro's many duties around the hacienda. Yet he lingered a few minutes, peering thoughtfully through the iron railing toward the distant hill. A secret rebellion against Don Luis had been pressing hard on Pedro's mind all day. The master had scolded him about nothing at all and he felt deeply hurt. He hadn't meant to snoop, but Don Luis had caught him squatting under the window of the manager's office, where he had no right to be. Don Luis had been talking in a very angry voice with Sebastian, the manager of his estate.

Something that his master had said to Sebastian had started Pedro thinking. "The hacienda could be in great danger and we must take all means to protect it. But not a word about this to anybody," Don Luis had ordered.

"That's why the gate has to be closed earlier," Pedro said to himself, pleased to have solved the riddle. But almost at once his face took on a troubled look. He was sorry he hadn't told his father about the danger to the hacienda. But his father was devoted to Don Luis and never questioned the will of his master. He was the overseer of the hacienda and had worked there all his life. There was no use. All he would get would be another scolding for his trouble.

Pedro sighed as he stood looking at the endless land that Don Luis owned, and his rebellion grew apace. Not one inch of all this land can my poor father call his own after so many years of working for the master, he thought, turning to look at Pinto as if to ask the dog if he didn't think so, too.

From the gate, Pedro could clearly see the hundreds of humble baked-mud huts where thousands of peons lived. They were practically all slave workers on the large estate; almost a small pueblo in itself. They had lived there all their lives and would die there, without once leaving the hacienda of Buena Vista.

He watched almost unseeingly the old women and the little girls making their endless trips from the brook to their huts, carrying jugs of water on their heads. Now and then they halted with their hands on their hips to stare at Pedro with secret envy. To be the overseer's son and to live behind the iron gate of the master was, indeed, a great privilege.

"If I only could run away and take my father with me!" Pedro said aloud, his sad eyes staring beyond the valley at the famous hill, the Chair of the Devil. The hill seemed at that moment to beckon to the boy to get away from the hacienda and have some adventures of his own.

"What say you, Pinto, you with the long legs, shall we run away?" Pedro asked his faithful dog as he embraced him.

The handsome hunting dog did not move an inch. His long, black-spotted white body was pressed tight against the earth, with his short tail pointing at a partridge he had spied.

Pedro shook his head sadly. "Even Pinto is a

slave worker for the master and thinks only of hunting for Don Luis," he said aloud with growing resentment.

A tall boy for his fourteen years, with suntanned cheeks and a winning smile, Pedro nevertheless was a shy boy who kept to himself and was happy only when alone with Pinto. Ever since he was ten years old he had been doing a man's work around the hacienda, with never a complaint about anything. His father was forever reminding him to look upon Don Luis as his lord and master, because he had been born on his hacienda and owed the master loyalty all his life.

"I've been patient with my lot of hard work and little food long enough; and with never a centavo to buy myself something I want!" Pedro spoke the words out loud, not caring who heard him.

With a gesture of defiance, he fingered the cheap rope that held up his long white cotton trousers. How he longed to buy a carved leather belt like the one Domingo, the master's son, wore when he came on vacation from his Military College in Chapultepec! Domingo had so many belts, and he had never had even one. Of course, it wasn't Domingo's fault. He would have given him one of his belts but he feared his father. He often spoke to him when Don Luis wasn't around; and once the young master had told him that when he graduated from the Military College he would take him to Mexico City as his personal servant.

A feeling of affection for Domingo made Pedro feel better. For Domingo he would do anything! He would wait patiently one or two or more years for Domingo.

A sudden, loud pat, pat, pat of a horse on the distant road drew Pedro's attention. He couldn't see the rider, but presently his sharp ears heard a softer pat of hoofs coming nearer, nearer to the side leading to the road in front of the gate. He looked toward the Chair of the Devil at the right of the road and saw a horseman making the turn to the Manor House. But still he couldn't see his face.

Pedro's heart beat fast. No one was allowed to come in through the master's gate without his permission. And at that hour! He drew away from the gate and with difficulty managed to drag unwilling Pinto away from his partridge. The dog would have remained pointing until someone killed it, and Pedro wanted no interference.

The horseman was galloping close to the gate now. Although this was the nearest thing to an adventure that Pedro had ever had in his life, he simply couldn't open that gate to anybody. He decided to run to the caretaker's cottage and tell his father. As he started running he heard the horseman calling him by name.

"Open the gate quickly, Pedro. Open, open the gate immediately!" The voice sounded familiar to Pedro, although it was very hoarse, and not exactly like the voice he thought he recognized.

"It is someone who knows me," he told himself and stopped running, listening attentively. He could hear the horseman calling again and again for him to open the gate; and the pounding at the iron railings.

¡Santa María Santísima! It is the master's son! Pedro recognized Domingo's voice.

A very tired young man almost fell over Pedro as Domingo dismounted from his horse. Pedro scarcely recognized him, disguised as he was in a cheap Indian blanket which he wore over his cadet uniform. Besides, the seventeen-year-old son of the master at that moment looked like a tired old man, with bent back and face disfigured by fatigue and the mud of the road.

"I've been riding this poor horse for ages, Pedro. Is my father at home?" Domingo leaned on Pedro, too tired to speak another word.

"The master is home," Pedro answered respectfully. It would have been rude to question Domingo directly, but he was thinking hard. Domingo was supposed to be at the Military College far, far away in Chapultepec. How could he ever have come on horseback all the way from the capital? The mule coach that brought the mail to the hacienda took days and days to come to Buena Vista.

"The coach broke down back in Monterrey and I hired one of the horses for the rest of the journey," Domingo told him.

"Poor master! His beautiful Arabian horse idle in the stable, and he had to ride on this bag of bones," Pedro answered, encouraged by Domingo's friendly talk.

The master's son was a short, fat youth, with light hair and eyes like his mother's, who was of Spanish ancestry. He was the only son of Don Luis and Doña Rosa and heir to the great estate. But Domingo was not like his parents, who kept proudly aloof from the servants. He was on very friendly terms with Pedro, whom he had known since his childhood, and he had a secret admiration for the humble Indian boy who always held his head high and feared no one, not even his masters.

Pedro wondered why Domingo had disguised himself in the Indian blanket. A master's son should never wear it under any circumstances, but he dared not ask. Instead, he quickly helped

Domingo to remove the poncho from the elegant cadet uniform and held the tired youth against his strong shoulders.

"I'm not sick, only very tired." Domingo was recovering his breath. "You don't know how many days and nights I've been riding this horse!" He threw the reins over Pedro's head, ordering him to take charge of the tired animal. "He must be dying of thirst, give him water. I'm all right now." He hastened across the courtyards to the Manor House, his ancestral home, that had been noted for its magnificence from the time of the conquistadors.

Up to this day, all his life, Pedro had obeyed his father and had never questioned anything that happened in the master's family. But this was different. The sudden arrival of Domingo, after what he had overheard earlier in the day, must have some special meaning. For the first time in his life, Pedro was ready to speak his mind to his father. He could scarcely wait to tell him everything.

After feeding the horse and leaving the animal comfortable in the stable, he ran to his cottage and lost no time in announcing to his father the arrival of the master's son, adding quickly,

"Something is happening at the hacienda and Don Luis doesn't want you to know it." Pedro continued before his father could stop him. "And the closing of the gate earlier has something to do with it. And the coming of Master Domingo without being expected has something to do with it also." He finished firmly, no longer afraid to discuss the master's private affairs with his father.

"In the name of all the saints, how do you know this?" his father asked in a whisper, as if fearing to be overheard.

Pedro told him what he had overheard Don Luis tell Sebastian, adding wisely, "If the hacienda is in danger we should know about it." He stepped out the door and pointed to the Manor House, which was all alight by the many oil lamps and chandeliers hanging from the ceiling. "If you permit me to take a little walk around there, I could find out *more*. You know how it is with the masters. They never tell us anything."

Old Gaspar looked at his son with an angry frown but controlled himself and did not answer. Presently he arose slowly and faced his son with pained eyes, holding his muscular hands in a gesture of helpless indecision. "I didn't bring a son into this world to be a traitor to . . ." Old Gaspar stopped himself and turned to pick up his *escopeta,* the ever ready shotgun he kept by the door, and walked out. "You stay inside and don't let me see you near the Manor House," he ordered as he walked away with bent head, deep in his own thinking.

Pedro watched his father go and wondered what he was going to do. Only once before had his father looked and acted as now. That had been during the revolution a few years before when Sebastian had compelled many of Old Gaspar's workers to go into the army against their will.

"*¡Caramba!* Why did I mention that Sebastian knew of the danger at the hacienda and didn't want my father to know it?" Pedro asked himself in desperation. He didn't mind a bit getting himself in trouble but his good old father! Why didn't his father let *him* have it out with Sebastian. He was younger, but he was already much taller and stronger than the manager, who was short and very thin.

Suddenly a loud gong resounded above Pedro's head. It was the master's bell calling his father to the Manor House. Pedro reached for the iron stick hanging by their own gong at the door and answered the call with the customary two bells, which was the signal that the overseer was not in his house but would be found immediately. Then he rushed out, calling his father frantically and running in the direction of Sebastian's own house, where Pedro thought his father had gone to fight with the manager.

Gasping and out of breath, Pedro reached Sebastian's house. It was completely dark. He called, but no one answered. He ran boldly now in the direction of the Manor House, thinking he had a good excuse to go, to say that his father was nowhere to be found.

"They will probably let me in this time." Pedro was full of hope as he prepared himself to answer the master's summons in his father's place.

But Pedro never got inside. As he was about to knock at the door, he heard the voice of Don Luis saying: "I know you can be trusted and I value your honesty and devotion but I am not so sure about Pedro." Don Luis raised his voice. "That *muchacho,* born within these walls, who owes me, his master, loyalty to the death, has been heard to express a desire to run away from the hacienda . . ."

Pedro stopped listening and tiptoed to the

French window to look inside the lighted room
and find out to whom the master was talking.
And there was his father! Standing before the
seated Don Luis, with his head bent as usual.

And there was Sebastian, and Domingo by the side of Doña Rosa, his mother, who seemed to have been weeping and was wiping her eyes. All the world was there but him! The private world of Don Luis summoned to hear about the danger to the hacienda! It was a good thing that no one had seen him, nor would any know that he had overheard Don Luis. And he would be careful to keep his hurt well hidden in his heart. But what was happening at the hacienda that Don Luis didn't want him to know about?

With great caution Pedro tiptoed away from the window, defeated and very angry.

"Blessed Lord, give me courage! Give me courage to face my father like a man and to defend myself!" he cried as he ran barefooted down to the courtyard and back to his cottage.

CHAPTER 2
The Americans Are Coming

AT the time of the American war with Mexico, back in the year 1847, the Mexican landowners still lived like the Spanish conquistadors who had ruled over the land for two centuries. They owned enormous haciendas—landed estates for farming or cattle raising—with thousands of native Mexican Indians working for them, ignorant of everything but their masters' wishes.

Don Luis Ramos Blancos was one of the richest of the landowners and he lived in great luxury and comfort. He was a tall, heavy-set man

16

with a deep voice that frightened everybody, except his family. He loved his wife, Doña Rosa, and his son Domingo, whom he was very proud to have studying at the exclusive Military College of Chapultepec, where only the sons of the rich and powerful were admitted. For the workers on his vast estate, Don Luis had little regard. Even the coins he paid them were his private hacienda pieces and of no value outside of his own pueblo of San Juan de la Buena Vista.

At the moment Domingo arrived unexpectedly at the Manor House, Doña Rosa, his mother, had just gone into the *sala* to play the harp for Don Luis, who liked to be lulled to sleep by the music.

The sudden sight of her son at the door startled Doña Rosa beyond words. She screamed and tripped over the gilded-wood harp, awakening her husband. And presently the great *sala* turned from a peaceful room into a chamber of grief and fears with the incredible news their son had brought them.

"But are you sure, my son, are you sure you know what you're saying?" Don Luis asked Domingo for the third time, walking up and down the long room with his hands clasped behind his back.

"Everything I told you I overheard my god-father himself tell the others," Domingo answered impatiently. "I don't know who the others were, they talked behind closed doors in the office of the College. But I know . . ."

Doña Rosa interrupted Domingo. "Our son is not telling fairy stories," she put in quickly, looking at her husband. "If his godfather says that the Americans are coming to raid the hacienda, they *are* coming. The general is in the confidence of Santa Anna, as you well know," Doña Rosa finished proudly.

"I know old Godfather has been with Santa Anna a long time," Don Luis said, trying to think of something. "I remember he was with him in the Battle of Veracruz, when the French fleet came to collect damages to French shop-keepers, and poor Santa Anna had one of his legs torn off by a French cannonball."

Domingo gave an impatient sigh. He wasn't interested in the Battle of Veracruz; he was interested in the danger to the hacienda. "Why don't you believe me, Papá?" Domingo asked. "I ran away from the College and came to tell you, to warn you, to save you and Mamá." He took out of his knapsack two newspapers. "Look, Mamá, look at these newspapers I brought from

Chapultepec. Read, read what they say." Domingo held the papers out to his mother.

Before Doña Rosa had time to take them, Don Luis snatched them from Domingo, looked at them hurriedly and handed them to Sebastian. "Read what they say!" he commanded roughly, too upset to read them himself.

One of them was a Mexican newspaper and the other an American. Sebastian looked at the American paper with a satisfied smile. He was proud that he knew English and Don Luis did not.

"Let us see what our Mexican paper says, first," Sebastian said tactfully, and started reading the page Domingo had marked.

"The American army is made up of Texas adventurers who have no country, no political or religious creed, no moral principles and there is nothing to fear from such people . . ."

"How true, how very true!" Don Luis interrupted excitedly. "Those Yanquis think they can frighten Mexico but they don't know our Indians! Our millions of patriots who are ready to die for their country!"

Doña Rosa paid no attention to her husband's

boasting and said, "Let us hear what the other newspaper says. It is the American paper, no?"

"Yes, Señora, it is *The Washington News* from the United States," Sebastian answered, losing no time in reading the English printing to himself, first, and then translating aloud into Spanish:

> "We must teach the Mexicans we are superior to them in energy as well as military skill . . . Must convince them that their interest is peace with the United States . . ."

Domingo interrupted, "You see, Papá, the Americans are threatening us! And my godfather knows the plans of the American Army, and knows definitely that the American General Zachary Taylor is coming to Buena Vista any time now . . ."

Don Luis had had about enough of Domingo's nonsense. He snatched from Sebastian the thin sheets of the Mexican paper, folded it and put it in his pocket. The American paper he tore angrily and threw it on the floor.

"Papá, Papá! There is more in the American paper you ought to know about," Domingo exclaimed, picking up the torn newspaper. "My godfather was reading from it to the others . . ."

But his father wasn't listening. He had taken Sebastian and Old Gaspar with him to the other end of the room and was whispering to them.

"Come with me to my room, Domingo, and bring the American paper," Doña Rosa said timidly, but determined to know what was in that paper. "Thank God you're studying English at the College," she told her son as they started out the room.

Sebastian stopped Doña Rosa. "Señora, please don't go. Don Luis wishes you to stay, and Domingo also. We have to make plans to defend the hacienda and he wants me to read more from *The Washington News*." The manager took the paper from Domingo.

"Blessed be the Lord!" Doña Rosa exclaimed with a smile. "One moment it is one thing and the next it is another with Don Luis."

"Silence!" Don Luis commanded of everybody, when he saw one of the servants coming in to announce that supper was ready. Then he spoke to Old Gaspar: "And you, my faithful overseer, listen to me. Go back to your work as usual, and not one word about all this to anybody. I don't wish the workers to know that the Americans are coming. They must know nothing, nothing at all."

Old Gaspar opened his mouth for the first time during the conference. "The master can trust his obedient servant," Pedro's father answered in a trembling voice. "You shall see who are the faithful when the time comes to . . ."

"I know your heart and I value your honesty, but watch out for that rascal Pedro. I suspect him to be on the side of the workers against his master. Now, go and teach that son of yours to do his duty." He pushed Old Gaspar out the door.

"God forbid! But if Pedro is a traitor I shall take care of him," the overseer said as he walked away.

"But Papá! You can trust Pedro. He is a good and a very intelligent *muchacho*. He can help us very, very much. I don't see why you feel like that about him," Domingo pleaded.

"Because I know these young Indians better than you do. They are beginning to question their masters." Don Luis turned away from Domingo to speak to Sebastian.

"And now let us hear what the American paper says," he commanded.

There was much in *The Washington News* to alarm even Don Luis: The forces of the American General Zachary Taylor had taken Saltillo—

and that was only about ten miles from Buena
Vista. On the coast, around the port of Veracruz,
one General Winfield Scott had taken several
towns. The American general was waiting for
orders from the American President Polk to advance on Mexico City.

Doña Rosa gave an uncontrolled scream. "To
the capital! To our City of Mexico, our only
refuge where we could be safe in case . . ."

"Lies! Nothing but Yanqui dreams of con-
quest of our country," Don Luis screamed back.

"They will never get near our beautiful capital."
He brushed off Sebastian's hands from the American paper and walked out of the *sala* into the dining room.

"To eat!" he shouted as he left the room. "Tomorrow will be another day." Don Luis repeated the Mexican proverb in a calmer tone of voice.

Doña Rosa, with Domingo and Sebastian, who always ate with the family, followed Don Luis into the dining room. No one seemed to be hungry except Don Luis; and Doña Rosa could no longer control her resentment.

"But why hasn't General Santa Anna sent word to *you* of all this?" she asked, not caring if the servants heard her.

"Precisely because *we* have nothing to fear for *ourselves*," Don Luis whispered in his wife's ear. "Santa Anna is our friend and protector and he knows how to handle the Yanquis. He will never permit our lands to be . . ."

"I suppose Santa Anna doesn't need conscripts from our hacienda, *this* time," Doña Rosa put in with an angry biting of her lips. "Only when Santa Anna needs you he remembers you are his friend."

A silence fell over the table. No one spoke for a long time and Doña Rosa and Domingo exchanged anxious glances with Sebastian, but neither of them dared question Don Luis about what was to be done to protect themselves from the Americans.

In the overseer's cottage another conference was taking place between father and son. When Old Gaspar returned to Pedro he was a broken man trying to make up his mind what to do about his son. Never before had he suspected Pedro of any wrongdoing but what else was there to think, now?

"I have tried to bring you up as a dutiful son to your father and a faithful servant to your master," Old Gaspar lamented, trying to control his anger.

"What have I done?" Pedro asked bravely, looking straight at his father's face.

"God only knows what you have done but the master suspects you of being a traitor. Have you been talking to the workers about wanting to run away from the hacienda?"

Pedro did not answer, but he didn't deny it either. "I always want to tell you everything but you never listen to me," Pedro said pleadingly. "You believe and you do only what Don Luis tells you, even when it is against your own wishes and against your son."

"Don't let me hear you speak so rudely about Don Luis again," Old Gaspar scolded, losing his temper completely. "From now on you will not leave the cottage without my permission. You will speak not one word, not one word to the workers; and you will come with me now to beg forgiveness of Don Luis." Old Gaspar gave the boy a vicious slap in the face and another, and another when Pedro refused to go.

At that moment the gong above their heads rang madly.

"The master's bell!" Old Gaspar let Pedro go and ran to the Manor House.

It was the first time his father had beaten Pedro and he was heartbroken. He wouldn't have cared if his father had beaten him for some deed of his own, but to be beaten for the sake of Don Luis! He watched Old Gaspar running through the courtyards until he disappeared, and a great resolution came to him. "Now is my chance and God give me courage to do it!" he said to himself. Taking his father's *escopeta,* which stood by the door, he walked cautiously to the gate and out of the Manor House grounds.

CHAPTER 3

Man Hunt for Pedro

THE morning light was already over the Manor House, making the courtyard look like a silver lake, but no one had thought of going to bed. Only Domingo had tried to take a nap at his mother's urgent pleading that he should rest after his long journey, but his young mind was too active and he couldn't sleep.

"Do you really think that we can get away from the hacienda without the workers hearing about it?" Domingo asked his mother, who was already packing.

"Hush, hush! Your father might hear you.

27

He is in the next room with Sebastian and Gaspar giving them his final orders."

Domingo gave a sleepy yawn, but hastened to put his ear to the closed door and tried to hear what they were saying. "They are talking about Pedro, and Old Gaspar is moaning and sobbing as if his heart would break," he announced, quite awake now.

"Never mind Pedro; he is the least of my anxieties," Doña Rosa whispered. "Let us finish packing the silver, dear son, our family heirlooms I adore!"

Domingo went back to packing carelessly the precious silver pieces inside a chicken crate. "But how do you think we can take all this with us?" he asked. "Don't you think there are more important things to think about than packing these old things!"

"We are *not* taking them with us, dear son of my life!"

"Then for what do we pack them?" Domingo promptly sat down, giving up the tiresome chore.

"Get on, get on with it, my angel! We are going to *bury* all our valuables in the . . ."

Doña Rosa didn't finish speaking. Don Luis and Sebastian were coming in.

"Before we do anything else we have to find that *muchacho*, that ungrateful Pedro who must be hiding in some worker's cottage and will betray us," Don Luis thundered.

"Does Pedro know about the Americans coming?" Domingo questioned his father anxiously.

"Old Gaspar says he didn't tell him," replied the father. "I bet one eye of my face that he knows we are abandoning the hacienda."

"Let *me* go to look for him," Domingo pleaded. "I know I can find him. I will ride around the hacienda and he will see me and come out to meet me." The anxious youth started to go out the door.

"No, no, no!" Don Luis stopped him. "I've given my orders to Gaspar. He is going to do what has to be done." Don Luis turned quickly to Sebastian.

"And you, go and inform the workers there is to be no work today, that their master gives them a holiday. Tell them it is in honor of Domingo's visit to the hacienda. And forbid them to leave their huts until evening."

"A good idea, no?" Sebastian said, looking at Doña Rosa.

"And don't forget about the fiesta tonight . . ."

"What fiesta?" Doña Rosa interrupted her husband.

Don Luis ignored his wife. "Let there be lots of fireworks and plenty of refreshments for everybody," he continued, pushing the manager out of the door.

"Everything is well planned now," Don Luis

said to his wife in a pleasant voice, sitting down by her side.

Domingo asked his father anxiously, "When are we leaving?"

"We leave tonight. Two coaches with our good mules will be waiting by the back road. We will be miles from here while the workers are singing and dancing like *locos!*" Don Luis announced with a chuckle.

The sound of a bugle horn calling startled Doña Rosa.

"The gatekeeper announcing someone coming in from the main gate," she exclaimed.

"Perhaps it is the post coach with letters!" Don Luis hurried out to look at the distant road. A solitary horseman was galloping madly to the Manor House.

It was a "runner-messenger." Mexico had no railroads, and runner-messengers, on flying post horses carried important communications between cities. Specially trained Indian youths and post horses rode incredible distances from post to post. The runner would hand the message to a fresh runner waiting at his own post, riding madly without even stopping his horse. The fresh runner would ride to the next town, deliver the message and return again to his post.

"A letter from your godfather from Chapultepec Castle!" Don Luis announced, extracting it from a packet of letters and newspapers the runner-messenger had brought.

The letter told of Domingo's disappearance from the Military College and of the anxiety over his absence. Domingo trembled a little. But Don Luis paid no attention and read the rest: Santa Anna had succeeded in convincing the American President Polk that he could restore peace in Mexico without the need of the American Army coming to the capital.

"To our Mexico City?" Doña Rosa exclaimed. "But the Yanquis are nowhere near there, or are they?" she asked, on the verge of tears.

"There is one American General Winfield Scott who has taken several cities around the coast, near Veracruz, and has now made his headquarters somewhere near Puebla!" Don Luis read to them.

"But the Americans will never, never get any further," Domingo said knowingly.

The barking of dogs with their guau . . ., guau . . ., guauuuú, made Doña Rosa jump. "What can that be?" she asked in alarm.

Don Luis took her by the arm and into the next room without explaining.

Sebastian walked out into the corridor as the four great house watchdogs were running after two of the Indian workers on horseback. "It is the man hunt for Pedro," he told Domingo casually.

"What! A man hunt for that poor boy!" Domingo couldn't believe such a thing.

"The master's orders. I can't interfere."

Domingo ran to the stable, ordered his Arabian horse, and rode straight to Old Gaspar's cottage. There he found the old man on his knees praying and weeping, and spoke to him quickly.

"I promise you they'll never get Pedro. Now, ask no questions. I want to take Pinto with me." Domingo called the dog, and Pinto came and stood at attention. He was used to going with Domingo on hunts.

"Where is Pedro?" Domingo asked, showing the dog Pedro's hat and rubbing it hard against his nose. "Now, Pinto, we are going to find Pedro. Where is he?"

Pinto, trained not to bark, could only show his joy and understanding by wagging his tail and jumping about, whimpering softly as he scratched the door trying to get out.

"Very well. Come on. Come, show me, where

is Pedro?" Domingo mounted his horse and
Pinto followed slowly, his nose to the ground.
He sniffed here and there, stopping now and
then, until at last he started running, so that it
was all Domingo could do to keep his horse
pacing after Pinto, who was disappearing now
and then in the corners of the crooked back road
that was rarely used by anyone.

At last the dog made a quick dash for a hut and stopped at the open door. Domingo dismounted and went in, happy to see that the place was in the opposite direction from where the man hunt was going on, although the voices of the fierce dogs were clearly heard.

The hut was abandoned. There was not a soul in sight. But Pinto had flattened himself on the rough earthen floor, whimpering joyfully.

"Now, where is Pedro? Where did he go from here, Pinto? Up, up and find Pedro, Pedro!"

Pinto sniffed all around. Had he been able to speak he would have said Pedro is in this house; no use going any further. As he could not speak, he whimpered softly and walked very slowly toward the back and stopped at a large opening in the ground. There Pinto flattened himself again and wouldn't be budged.

Domingo, puzzled, looked inside the hole. It was the entrance to a sort of cave and without hesitation he went in.

There was Pedro, trembling because he did not know what the son of the master might do to him. In tears, he fell on his knees and kissed Domingo's hand.

"Never mind that. I have come to save you, Pedro. There is a man hunt on for you."

"I know. I heard the dogs and the call of the horn. *We* could see them riding toward the Chair of the Devil, where they always have the man hunts for the prowlers."

"Who are 'we'? Is anyone else here with you? Does anyone know you are hiding here?"

"No. I am alone. But two of the oldest
workers, very good friends of mine, live here.
They have gone to spread the news to the men
at the Chair of the Devil, that they saw me riding away on a mule during the night. God bless
them and forgive them for the lie they had to
tell!"

"Fear not, Pedro, I will protect you. Stay here
until I return."

Domingo mounted his horse and looked
around for Pinto. But Pinto had disappeared
inside the cave, happy to be with Pedro, and
Domingo had no time to waste. He rode in the
direction of the Chair of the Devil and met the
two Indian men in charge of the man hunt.

"*¡Basta!* Enough! I know where Pedro is. The
rascal has run away on a mule during the night.
Take the dogs back. I shall notify your master."

The day passed quickly for Don Luis and
Doña Rosa, with all that had to be done for the
escape to Mexico City. Don Luis had read again
the godfather's letter to his wife and they had
enjoyed part of it immensely.

"I told you that Santa Anna is too clever for
the Yanquis. Our one-legged general is worth
one hundred of the American generals with two
legs."

"But ten thousand dollars, American?" It seemed that Santa Anna had asked for that amount from President Polk and the money had been sent to him. "And the Americans gave the money on Santa Anna's word he would use it to put an end to the revolution and pacify the country?" Doña Rosa shook her head.

"You don't like Santa Anna, do you?" Don Luis snapped angrily. "He is a great patriot, and the Americans are very, very rich. They want our country, no? Let them pay for it."

But this was no time for quarreling. Godfather had arranged for a military escort somewhere on the road, had arranged for their stay for the nights at the houses of the governors of the states they had to cross. So happy and relieved they had been that both had taken a good siesta.

Evening came. Old Gaspar had his orders. After the family left it was he who would remain in complete charge of the hacienda. He was the faithful overseer left to protect the ancestral home and die defending it if necessary, when the Yanquis came.

Soon after sunset, great fireworks began to burn, throwing clusters of stars and golden threads of fire in the air. At the very gate of the

Manor House an enormous *castillo*—a castle—
of fireworks had been built. The fiesta was at its
height with the workers singing and playing
their *bandurrias* and balancing themselves on
one foot from the abundant refreshment in
honor of the son of the master's visit.

It was then, about the time the great *castillo*
was burning, that a little group of people were
getting inside the two coaches, drawn by four
mules each, waiting by the family's private back
road.

In the first coach was Sebastian, the manager, and two servants, a woman and a man, all well armed, sitting between crates of clothing and of food and wines and some large Spanish leather chests.

In the second coach, with cushions and three mattresses, rode Don Luis and Doña Rosa and Domingo, in as much comfort as possible, and protected by the coach in front, in case of some mishap on the road.

The mules trotted quickly away. They were preferred to horses for such a journey. Nothing better than mules for the broken sod of the many canyons they would come to. The sure-footed animals were soon over the narrow path by the bank of the stream and miles from the Manor House.

"Thank all the saints we are on our way to safety!" Doña Rosa exclaimed, while Domingo tucked his mother inside the soft cushions and wrapped around her a large Spanish shawl.

Don Luis grinned at his wife and son silently, but he was thinking, "There is no use fooling myself. The American war with Mexico is something to think about, and God help us!"

CHAPTER 4

Liberty or Death

THE bells of the church in the village were ringing softly, like distant voices whispering hope and faith in a world full of sorrow. Pedro stood behind the door of the hut where he had been hiding with Pinto all night without sleeping a wink. Impatiently he listened closely for some sign of life in the hacienda, but there wasn't a sound.

He peeped out of the door but couldn't see a single worker in the fields. It must be reaching noon; he could tell by the shadows made by the sun over the huts.

41

"The whole world is keeping very quiet, waiting for us to show up and catch us, eh, Pinto?" he asked his dog, picking up the shotgun and fingering it with a confident gesture. With such a fine *escopeta* Pedro felt ready for anything.

"For me it is liberty or death." He spoke out loud to himself, as people often do when they are alone with their secret thoughts.

He hadn't seen a soul since Domingo had come with Pinto. The two old people, Juan and Guadalupe, who lived in the hut, had stayed away, too. He wondered why the son of the master had not returned as he had promised, and how much longer he should wait for him.

He couldn't wait forever! In his impatience, Pedro's mind suddenly cleared. "That is *it!*" he exclaimed. "Domingo must be still asleep, and the workers always sleep all day after a fiesta." He told himself this with renewed hope for his safety, remembering the music and the singing he had heard during the night, and the fireworks that had illumined the sky over the Manor House.

That had not surprised him. There always was a fiesta for the son of the master when he came home from his Military College.

"But where is my father? He never sleeps late. Can it be he has gone to the hills in search of me?" Pedro realized that he was wasting precious time. Why not sneak out now while everybody slept, go by the deserted back road, reach the corral, take one of the horses, and with God's help be off and away to freedom.

"What do you say, Pinto?" Pedro bent down and embraced the dog.

But Pinto did not budge. Standing very stiff with his long, flat ears alert and tail in the air, Pinto was giving Pedro another one of his hunting signals.

Pedro followed Pinto's tail with his eyes and saw three people walking through the thick bushes in the distance. *"Bien*—very well!" Pedro acknowledged the dog's warning.

Long before the three people reached the door, Pedro was out in the courtyard, shotgun in hand, bravely waiting for anything.

Old Gaspar burst into tears of remorse for the beating he had given his son, muttering Indian words of affection and pity.

"There's no need to feel sorry for me." Pedro faced his father without emotion. "I've made up my mind about what I want to do."

"But you don't know what has happened,

Pedro," Juan and Guadalupe, who accompanied Gaspar, put in quickly. "The master abandoned the hacienda last night and we're all alone now."

"You're trying to fool me! You're going to turn me in to Don Luis," Pedro said with an angry frown.

"No, my son! Listen to your father. I should have told you yesterday about the danger to the hacienda but . . ."

"But what *was* it, what *was* it?" Pedro interrupted impatiently.

"The Yanquis are coming to raid Buena Vista, and Dios help us!" the two old people said in one frightened voice. "And that's why the master has gone away."

Pedro opened his mouth in surprise. Then suddenly a great idea came to him and he gave a loud Indian yell of joy. But still he wasn't telling anybody what he was thinking.

He stood before his father for some moments, his head reeling with new thoughts and secret plans. After hearing the tremendous news, Pedro at that moment had grown up many years. From a youth of fourteen he was now an *hombre,* a free and intelligent adult with definite plans to execute.

Presently, with blurred eyes, he spoke in a

new, slightly hoarse voice, "Who said that the Americans are coming to raid the hacienda?" he asked Juan and Guadalupe.

"Domingo brought the news and the newspapers that tell of war with the United States," Juan said.

"And it was Don Luis himself who told your father," Guadalupe put in.

"And when did Don Luis say that the Americans were coming to Buena Vista?" Pedro addressed his father this time.

"Dios help us! I don't know that, my son. No one knows, but the Yanquis may come any time, at nightfall, even this evening." Old Gaspar moaned.

Pedro bit his lips to hide a smile of satisfaction. "Then we have to prepare to defend the hacienda," he said slowly.

"That's what has to be done," the father said, "and we have to tell all the workers. They know nothing, nothing of this. They will get frightened and run away to the hills."

Pedro reflected a moment. "Where is Sebastian, the manager?" he asked.

"Sebastian went away with the master, also . . ."

"So!" Pedro gave a savage laugh. "We shall

see now who are the brave and who the true patriots."

"But what are you thinking?" his father asked.

"God will see to that," Pedro replied. "I know many, many workers here who will not run away to the hills after I talk to them. They want their liberty from the master as much as I do."

"Pedro is right, and we are with Pedro," both Juan and Guadalupe announced, ignoring their overseer for the first time in their lives.

"In the name of Dios, are you all gone *locos* also?" Old Gaspar said in a commanding tone. "Don Luis left *me* in charge of the hacienda. You will do as I say. Master's orders."

"Master's orders!" Pedro repeated with a mocking gesture. "It is always master's orders, even after Don Luis has abandoned us like dogs!"

Old Gaspar bent his head and said nothing. He was beginning to think he had had enough of Don Luis, too; and yet what could Pedro do? Surely the workers would not listen to him, so young and ignorant, although he had to acknowledge, as he looked at the tall and strong boy before him, that Pedro looked more like twenty than fourteen, and was talking like an *hombre*.

"And what are you going to say to the workers?" he asked.

"I said that we shall see what we shall see," Pedro answered, turning to face the two old people. "You are with me, no?"

"Yes. And your father is with you, also." They spoke for Old Gaspar, who was about to collapse with fear for his son's safety in his mad enterprise, whatever it was.

"Then, Juan, you go to all the men, wake everybody up, tell them the Americans are coming to raid the hacienda, and they are to come to the Manor House. Tell them I have a secret plan by which we shall all be saved and made free. Tell them not to be afraid of the Americans . . ."

"And the women and children? Can they come to the Manor House, too?" asked Guadalupe.

"Oh, yes. Ask everybody to come. I shall be there to speak with all who wish to hear me," Pedro said, looking straight at his father. "As for you, good father, do as you please. Only tell me this. Where are those newspapers that tell of war with the United States?"

"*¡Ay, ay, ay!*" Old Gaspar exclaimed. "I'm glad you reminded me. Don Luis asked me to burn them and I forgot. They must be still on the floor in the master's room."

Pedro ran to the Manor House without another word.

Seated in the center of the courtyard before a handsome table that he had dragged out from the Manor House, Pedro looked over the workers squatting here and there and everywhere around him. Only a few hundred of the thou-

sands of workers on Don Luis's enormous estate had answered his call.

But with the intuition of youth, Pedro had not made a mistake. They had responded quickly to the message from the overseer's son, whom everybody liked and trusted. Frightened by the incredible news of the expected raid on Buena Vista by the American soldiers and the departure of the master, Pedro's message had stirred the hearts of the long-suffering peons, in spite of their well-grounded fear for their lives.

Not even when Juan and Guadalupe an-

nounced there was panic at the hacienda, with hundreds of Indian families already packing their belongings on donkeys and mules and horses, did these selected workers lose faith in Pedro.

"What did the workers say they are going to do?" Pedro asked the two old people.

"Some are going to hide in the hills and others are riding to near-by villages for safety," Juan and Guadalupe announced.

"Let them go, let those poor slave workers have a taste of freedom, no matter what else happens to them," Pedro said with rare wisdom. "They will probably return when they hear what I intend to do."

To the faithful squatting in front of him, Pedro was now talking as they had never been spoken to before. Men, women and children listened with their mouths open, amazed at Pedro, the overseer's son who was now their friend and protector.

"From the mule drivers who come to get the produce from the hacienda I have heard what is going on outside Buena Vista." Pedro told them. "There is another revolution and that's why the Americans are coming. But the Americans are on the side of the workers!" Pedro exclaimed in a voice full of fire and rebuke at Don Luis's actions. "When the American soldiers come to the hacienda, I shall tell them everything and they will listen to me."

"Tell them, tell the Yanquis how every year at harvesttime Don Luis promised to give us a little piece of ground for ourselves, but after the harvest he gave us nothing, nothing," some of the women in the crowd pleaded.

"That I will do, and much more . . ." Pedro stopped to look at a group of people coming through the gate of the Manor House.

It was his father with the village priest, followed by a number of women and children. Pedro remained standing, holding his head high. But the workers knelt on the ground as the padre passed through the crowd, and some kissed his hand, as was their custom.

The padre addressed Pedro, "My son, I've come to give you my benediction." The padre made the sign of the cross over Pedro, who stood before him. "We will defend the hacienda like good patriots, if necessary. But perhaps, God willing, it won't be necessary."

Pedro handed the padre the newspapers he had found in Don Luis's room.

"These newspapers tell of the Americans

coming to raid the hacienda, but as you know, good padre, no one here can read. Please read them to us!" Pedro pleaded.

The padre took the papers but didn't read them. "I know everything that is in them," he said, as he looked at the dates, which were a couple of weeks old. "I will tell you all you have to know, and you, my sons, must have faith in God."

"Do not be afraid," the padre continued. "Fear is bad. As long as we do what is good and just there should be no room in our hearts for fear. The American soldiers will soon be here, that's true, but they are not savages . . ."

Pedro had to interrupt. He stood straight and unafraid before the priest, and said in a decisive voice: "I've heard that the Americans are on the side of the workers and against the masters. I am a Mexican and love my country, but I am a worker and we here all are workers and . . ." He stopped for a moment to look at his father, but decided to say what he felt he had to say. "I am for fighting against the cruel masters on the side of the Americans!"

Cries of approval from the crowd filled the courtyard. "We are with Pedro, we are against Don Luis!" Their voices drowned the padre's words and they would not stop until the padre made the sign of the cross over them.

"General Santa Anna has a very large army near here," the padre told them. "My advice to everybody is to remain quiet at the hacienda until the soldiers of the American General Zachary Taylor come. *If* they can get through." The padre stopped and made a warning gesture with his index finger in the air, then continued. "Santa Anna, with the tricks of a rattlesnake, is ready to meet the Americans, to ambush them in the narrow Pass of La Angostura!"

"In La Angostura?" Pedro repeated. "But that is only two miles from Buena Vista!" He made a mental note of this important fact so he wouldn't forget it.

"Santa Anna is a wicked and ambitious man," the padre went on, "not a brave soldier. He knows that the narrow Pass of La Angostura is so broken up into deep barrancas, hollows, ravines and precipices, made by centuries of rain and melting snow from the mountains, that neither artillery nor cavalry could ever get through. However, I happen to know that the forces of General Taylor are at this very moment advancing on to San Juan de la Buena Vista from the opposite side of Saltillo."

A great shout of relief came from sad and fearful throats.

"Now, remember all I have said. Don't be afraid. Go back to your huts, go back to work on your fields, make your houses neat and have everything in order for the Americans to see we are good people," the padre told the peons. Turning to Pedro, he said, "Something tells me that you, my son, were born for some great destiny."

After this, the good padre started away and as he reached the gate, to which Pedro had accompanied him, he turned and said, "If you need me, come to me. I am always with you, in the name of God."

CHAPTER 5

Here Come the Americans!

LATE in the afternoon of February 20, 1847, a detachment of General Zachary Taylor's army marched on San Juan de la Buena Vista. It was a small force of five thousand men but well equipped, with an imposing number of guns drawn by horses, a large gun crew and many officers on horseback. They had made the long miles from Saltillo without interruption or mishap, and at last the American Army was on the dirt road leading straight to Buena Vista.

General Taylor had followed the stream to the west of the road until they reached the safe valley. When Buena Vista was at last in sight, he sighed with relief.

55

"I've led my men exactly to the opposite end of the Pass of La Angostura," the general told himself. "Santa Anna's forces will be advancing to meet me from the other end of the pass." He felt quite sure about it.

He was planning already the position of his troops along the two-mile-wide valley. "I couldn't ask for anything better," he said, looking at the Sierra Madre Mountains which flanked the valley on both sides.

"I shall place the Fourth Artillery with Major John Washington's battery of guns on the narrow point of the valley. And flanking Washington, right on the ridges by the road, I'll have the First and Second Illinois regiments."

He sat comfortably on his horse, Old Whitey, and lit a cigar. "The rest of the army will be placed as need be," he decided finally.

In a confident mood, Taylor turned Old Whitey to face the Saltillo Road and gazed long at his army marching. "I still have the Texas Volunteers, the Kentucky and Arkansas cavalry, my Indiana Brigade, not forgetting the batteries of Sherman and Bragg. And my dragoons!" He chewed hard at his cigar. The general had a warm spot in his heart for his dragoons.

Once more he turned Old Whitey, with an

affectionate pat, and rode ahead in front of his army.

It had been hard going for the cavalry and artillery in a land without roads, but not for "Old Rough and Ready," as Taylor had been nicknamed for his forty years of service in Indian warfare. He was pleased with his peaceful advance, and felt decidedly relieved about having disobeyed orders from Washington.

General Taylor had political ambitions, for he was a candidate for President of the United States, and the orders he had received, Taylor thought, were intended to keep him in obscurity.

"Old Rough and Ready" had boldly moved down to Saltillo, and then come to San Juan de la Buena Vista on one of his famous personal hunches.

"They don't know, down there in Washington, as much as I do about these Mexicans and Indians," the general was thinking aloud as he rode. To appease the High Command he had sent a large detachment of his men on to General Winfield Scott, who was his rival for the Presidency of the United States.

"If only I had sent General Wool, also!" he told himself. But Wool had come with him, worse luck. He did not like Wool's ideas, at all. "I reduced my forces, but the men I have will be more than enough." Taylor looked affectionately at his soldiers over his shoulders, to the right and left of the long columns, particularly at his dragoons.

Some of these dragoons were the only survivors of that fatal April of the year before, 1846, when they had been ambushed and almost destroyed by Mexican cavalry. Taylor intended to see that this did not happen again. True, he in turn had defeated the Mexican General Arista the following month, and crossed the Rio Grande, taking his troops in river boats, sailing four hundred miles to Monterrey, and finally capturing Matamoros!

At the moment, however, "Old Rough and Ready" would rather forget about Matamoros. It had been a nice victory, but thousands of his men had died from an epidemic of measles and dysentery.

A stout man in his sixties, with untidy gray hair and wearing his famous green coat and cap and very wrinkled trousers, General Zachary Taylor made a striking contrast as he rode by the side of the younger general, John Wool. In a well-fitted blue tunic, with his epaulets shin-

ing bright, General Wool rode on his gray horse
with a trifle too dignified an air for Taylor's way
of thinking. That wasn't *his* way of touching a
soldier's heart!

And his way must have been the right way,
for it was Taylor whom the men worshiped; his
soldiers would follow him anywhere. Without a
fancy uniform with medals, he was a real commander. All his long years he had been an
Indian fighter, and until recently he had commanded a real army in a real battle. Untrained

as he was, he had already proved his skill at commanding troops in the three main branches of the army: the infantry, artillery and cavalry.

Outspoken and fatherly, "Old Rough and Ready" didn't hesitate to tell his men what he thought of this war with Mexico. Particularly to his favorite sergeant, whom he had nicknamed "Rough" because of a certain resemblance to his own ways. In Sergeant Rough, Taylor had found great natural skill in instructing recruits and in keeping order at quarters, as well as a friendly disposition toward the men in the small detachment he commanded.

To Sergeant Rough, Taylor talked very frankly as they were nearing their destination. He wanted to inspire his young sergeant with faith and purpose in the coming battle of Buena Vista, and at the same time to tell him what he thought of this Mexican "scrimmage," as he called it.

"The war with Mexico is a mess, and it has dragged on too long, unnecessarily long," the general told his sergeant.

"Yes, General." The sergeant answered short, knowing that his commander liked to talk at length.

"As a matter of fact, the war actually began on

April 25, 1845, when Congress agreed to the annexation of Texas."

"I remember, General." Rough answered with a grin, although he really didn't remember.

"Sure, sure you remember, Rough," the general winked at him suspectingly. "It was when President Polk ordered troops to the frontier and put me in command of the American troops there."

"That's what I was about to say, General, really." Rough couldn't help having a good laugh on himself.

"Well, the Mexicans thought it was an invasion of their country and the Mexican General Santa Anna started playing his little tricks. Now you have it." Taylor finished with something under his breath he'd rather Rough didn't hear him say.

Two years of cuddling Santa Anna had been far too long. And it was a mystery to Taylor why President Polk had permitted the Mexican general to return from exile in Veracruz. Yet, at the moment, as he talked to Sergeant Rough, Taylor remembered more than ever that faith and purpose were the true strength of a commander. When he finally reached the hacienda of Buena Vista, "Old Rough and Ready" was full of both faith and purpose, and with a strong hunch that the coming battle could be the end of Santa Anna.

Pedro, in the meantime, had taken charge of the hacienda and there wasn't any doubt about it. Two days only had he had in which to do the million things and to think the many million thoughts that kept jumping to his mind, demanding immediate execution.

The moment the padre had left, Pedro had advised everybody to go and do exactly what the padre had asked them to do. So the workers had gone to work on their fields, the women to tidy up their huts, and anyone coming through the hacienda would have found the life of the place very much the same as it had been before Don Luis and his family had abandoned it.

With one exception. The Manor House had been transformed. Pedro and his father had moved in, with the wives and children of some of the workers, who were a little sick and more than a little frightened. These sick ones had brought their straw mats upon which they were used to sleeping, and their Indian stones on which to cook and to grind their corn. They brought their pet cats and parrots and their hens and roosters, not forgetting their husbands' *bandurrias*—old stringed instruments resembling mandolins—without which no Mexican is happy.

Pedro welcomed the transformation of the elegant and forbidden Manor House into an Indian worker's home, nearly every inch of which was now covered by straw mats over Don Luis's precious Spanish carpets. He was amused when he saw chickens coming into Doña Rosa's music room and roosting on her harp.

But that had been the first day. That night, when Pedro retired to Domingo's room, which he had taken for his own because of his great affection for the son of the master, he took counsel with himself. In the silence of the night, he came to definite conclusions as to what must be done before and after the Americans came.

The first thing he thought about was what the good padre had said about him—that he had been born for some great destiny. In his secret heart Pedro agreed with him, humbly in a way, because he wasn't of a boasting nature, but he felt certain he was on the brink of a great adventure.

The second thing Pedro thought about was that his father had not said a word to him about his intention of going over to the side of the

Americans and to fight against Don Luis and all unjust masters. He decided he must begin at once to prepare the hacienda and the workers for the coming of the Americans. As yet, he hadn't the slightest idea when that would be.

"God will say what is to be done tomorrow," he told himself. Then, feeling exhausted both in body and mind, he looked around Domingo's room with a guilty feeling. What would Domingo think of him if he knew he had slept in his bed? Pedro wondered.

"No, no!" he told himself. "I must respect the son of the master even if only God sees me." With longing eyes turned toward the comfortable and elegant bed, Pedro stretched his straw mat on the floor and instantly fell sound asleep.

Had Pedro known when he awoke the following morning that the Americans would come that day, he could have saved himself a lot of work and not a little trouble. But he didn't, and his first thought on awakening was about General Santa Anna who, as the padre had told him, was only two miles away!

"The hacienda must be defended from Santa Anna's soldiers if they raid it before the Americans come!" Pedro was now commanding his army of workers. He felt like a general and had decided to make soldiers of his volunteer-recruits. Already he had given many, many orders. One of them was to remove all the doorknobs from the Manor House and make bombs of them. He had broken into Don Luis's storehouse, where the ammunition and the firearms were kept ready for the master's personal defending army when revolutions came near the Manor House.

In the storehouse, Pedro had found plenty of arms and much ammunition but no bombs, and he wanted a million of them. "Here is the dynamite!" he shouted triumphantly to the recruits, who were already helping themselves to small arms and dancing with joy at finding themselves soldiers instead of slave workers.

"Give me some of the dynamite, please, Pedro!" the fifteen-year-old Lupe, niece of Old Guadalupe begged, half in fear and half in delighted bravado.

Soon Lupe was sitting on the ground, making dynamite bombs out of the doorknobs stolen from the Manor House. She seldom moved her eyes from Pedro, except to make faces at the dog, Pinto, who never left his side and received all her young hero's affection.

Late in the afternoon Pedro had a larger army than he had expected. Besides the hundreds who had answered his call, many other workers who had run away had returned. The padre had gone in search of them and had talked them into going back.

"Now I go to see what my father is doing," Pedro told his soldiers, who were squatting all over the courtyards polishing their small arms, practicing their shooting, using as targets Don Luis's best sombreros. Others were helping Lupe with the homemade bombs.

Pedro had selected his father for the important post of *guardia*—watchman in the lookout tower of the Manor House, and had presented him with Don Luis's magnificent spyglass. But it was many hours since he had left him there and, being the siesta hour, Pedro wanted to make sure his good father had not fallen asleep.

"Sleep!" Pedro said to himself, when he heard his father yelling as he descended the stairs from the tower. "No danger of him sleeping. He's too excited."

"They're here, my son, they're here on the dirt road, not more than a mile away. The Americans are coming. And what an endless line of soldiers! And you never heard of so many wagons on the road at one time, and millions, millions of men in them and on horses . . ."

Pedro had not stopped to listen. He ran up to the tower, and the field glass showed him what he had longed to see.

He descended the stairs three at a time, with the haste of one about to do something on which his very life depended. He ran to the courtyard.

"The Americans are here!" He had to stop because panic and disorder were plainly shown in every face. "I know how you all feel. I feel the same. We are Mexicans and love our land. We shall behave like brave *hombres*. I believe the Americans are good people but . . ."

His father interrupted. "But if the Yanquis begin shooting and try to burn the hacienda before you have time to speak, and when you speak they do not listen to you, what then?" Old Gaspar was once more asserting his authority over his son.

"Then we shall defend the hacienda!" Pedro shouted, and ordered everybody to follow him out of the Manor House.

Quicker than one could have believed, the Manor House was emptied of every man, woman and child. The men carried their arms, and Lupe the box of dynamite on her head, as untroubled as if she were carrying a basket of fruit.

"To the *subterráneo*—the secret underground!" Pedro called. This was Don Luis's secret road that led to the hills.

"Here we shall wait and see what the Americans do," Pedro told them, when they were all safely in. Then he left them there and went out into the open spaces to think over this tremendous adventure that had come to him.

Night came. By now not only the Manor House had been transformed once more but the entire hacienda, all along its many miles. Barracks, temporary hospitals, headquarters for General Taylor and his officers, soldiers' tents everywhere here and there under the trees. In short, the encampment of the American Army at Buena Vista had been placed in a few hours. Taylor and Wool, with other officers, had retired to their headquarters in the Manor House to make final plans for the coming battle. But the soldiers were in a happier mood. Already they were preparing their campfires and making merry around them, eating and singing their favorite song, "Green Grow the Rushes, O!"

It was then, when the American soldiers were singing their "Green Grow . . ." over and over again, that Pedro crept out from under the thick bushes from which he had been watching the Americans. He had seen everything they did with growing amazement. Cautiously, he ran to the underground *subterráneo* to report to his anxious father and his volunteer army.

"No shooting, not one shot, and no burning of the hacienda!" he announced. "I'm for presenting ourselves to the Americans now, tonight."

A great hush fell over the workers, but no one objected. Only Old Gaspar spoke. "I will go with you. I want to be with my son wherever he goes and see what he does."

"Everybody here will go with me," Pedro said, and corrected himself. "All the men, that is. The women and children can go back to their huts, as there is nothing to fear." Without waiting for an answer, he led the men straight to the Manor House.

"There's that Mexican boy who has been prowling around, and how did he get in here?" General Taylor remarked when he saw Pedro walking in the courtyard of the Manor House where the general was sitting with his officers. "Let him come, and see what he wants," he told his aide-de-camp, who spoke Spanish.

Pedro was alone. He had changed his mind about bringing his army of volunteers until he spoke with the general in command, and with no one else.

"I come to speak with the general," Pedro said to the aide-de-camp.

"About what?" the aide asked in Spanish, to Pedro's delight.

"Oh, you speak like us!" he remarked to the aide, with great satisfaction. "Do me the favor to take me to the general," he begged, without answering his question.

"Okay," the aide said when he saw that Taylor was nodding to him to bring the young Mexican.

"No, no, please!" Pedro pleaded when he found himself standing in front of General Taylor. "It is the *general* I want to see. Only the general."

General Taylor's good-natured face broke into a broad grin. He guessed that the young Mexican had expected to see him in a magnificent uniform with many medals and had taken him for a nobody.

"Take him to Sergeant Rough," Taylor ordered the aide. "I like his face; see what he wants."

"What do you want to see the general about? And why didn't you speak to him? *That* was General Zachary Taylor, in command of the American Army," the aide said in a friendly manner.

Pedro glared at the aide. He wanted to say you are deceiving me, *that* was not the great American general. He wanted to say many things, but being a well-brought-up young man he said nothing. Instead, he asked the aide to excuse him the mistake he had made in his ignorance of American generals.

"No harm done. The general asked me to take you to Sergeant Rough. See you don't make any more mistakes."

Pedro nodded his head, and followed the aide with growing reassurance.

Sergeant Rough was a tall, heavy man in his early forties, humorous and resourceful, one of the Texas Volunteers who spoke Spanish very well.

"I came to offer myself and my volunteer army of workers in this hacienda to the general," Pedro said to Sergeant Rough without hesitation. "We are Mexicans and good patriots, but we are against Don Luis and we want to fight on the side of the Americans . . ."

"And who is Don Luis?" asked Sergeant Rough.

Pedro told his tale of woe to the sergeant, who listened not a little amazed but quite pleased. These natives with a grudge against their masters could be very useful, indeed, Rough was thinking.

"How old are you?" Rough asked Pedro suddenly.

"I am going to twenty years," Pedro lied soberly. "But many of my men are even older. We all ride very well and all Mexicans know how to shoot."

"Follow me," Rough said to Pedro, and led him into his private quarters.

At the door were two horses tied to a tree, and inside was a rider that Rough hadn't expected back so soon. He had sent out two of his men to observe possible enemy movements.

"Corporal Andrews was ambushed and captured by Santa Anna's men," the soldier who had returned safely announced to Sergeant Rough. "But I managed to save the horse . . ."

"What did he say about Santa Anna?" Pedro interrupted, addressing Rough before he had time even to think.

"You keep quiet!" Sergeant Rough pushed

Pedro away from him, and continued speaking to the soldier.

Pedro couldn't understand a word of English, but every time Santa Anna was mentioned he jumped from his chair and tried to speak. He had divined exactly what had happened. He knew that a horse brought in without his rider meant the horseman had been killed or captured by Santa Anna.

"I can show the *safe* roads to ride all the way to La Angostura!" Pedro said out loud, trying to draw attention to himself.

"What did you say?" Sergeant Rough asked.

"Is it about Santa Anna's headquarters you want to know?" Pedro asked eagerly. "That I can find out as easy as catching a fly. I can walk the two miles there on hidden roads and spy around until I find Santa Anna's eight-mule coach and his fighting cocks, those he always takes to battle with him." Pedro stood tall and straight and impatient to start on his daring trip to Santa Anna's headquarters.

"What are you talking about? What is all this about an eight-mule coach and fighting cocks? Have you gone loco?"

"Everybody knows about Santa Anna's fighting cocks. He always takes them in crates to bat-

tle for good luck. He calls them his generals!"
Pedro explained.

Sergeant Rough had never heard about the
fighting cocks, but was thinking over what Pedro
had said. Turning to one of his corporals, he remarked, "It is little things like this that sometimes save lives, although it sounds silly." He
turned to Pedro and gave him a friendly pat on
the back.

Pedro stared at Sergeant Rough with eyes
shining with joy. Quickly he said, "I could go
now, in the night, and find out for you exactly
where Santa Anna has his headquarters . . ."

"Come with me," Sergeant Rough interrupted. "We'll see what the general thinks."

CHAPTER 6

Pedro's Dream Comes True

B Y the light of the moon, Pedro started walking, headed for the hidden roads he knew would take him safely to La Angostura and Santa Anna's headquarters. He looked back to give a last good-by to Sergeant Rough, who had come with him to learn which was the hidden road he was talking about.

"Don't forget what I told you, Pedro," Rough called when he saw him disappearing down a steep incline in the earth that was so overgrown by bushes that no one would have taken it for a road leading anywhere.

76

"I shall remember everything the sergeant told me, but I'll find Santa Anna's camp in my own way," Pedro told himself. He made for the foothills through incredibly thick bushes, on all fours like a cat.

He was glad he had not listened to Sergeant Rough about wearing the soldier's boots he had been given, and the blue coat which was now the uniform of Lookout Pedro. The sergeant had said:

"Wear your boots, Pedro, and save your feet."

"Well, if I had, I couldn't go half as fast, nor could I jump over the rocks like a goat, or cross the brook like a fish. And that's how it has to be done." He kept talking to himself and thinking hard.

How could he go to spy on Santa Anna dressed in the elegant uniform of the American soldier? This he had thought out by himself, without mentioning it, and had changed into his white cotton pants and shirt, carrying his poncho over one shoulder and his *lazo* tied around his waist. This way he was no longer an American soldier, but just a peon, in case, just in case he met somebody on the way.

Sergeant Rough knew nothing of this. Pedro had hidden his Mexican clothes under the bushes of the hidden road and had waited for Sergeant Rough to ride away before he changed.

"I hope some animal doesn't do anything to this beautiful uniform," Pedro thought as he folded it very carefully and covered it with wide, thorny cactus leaves. "I want to find you just as I left you." He talked to the uniform as he placed a very tall, thick bamboo stick in the earth near by, with some enormous red cactus flowers he had tied at the end of the stick with strong ribbon grass.

The path Pedro was taking now, cautiously because it was open space and the moon was shining bright over his head, was a path that took him straight to the creek. He stopped and went inside a hollow place made by the water, folded his poncho small and tied it on top of his head with his *lazo*. Then he crossed the little river, swimming very quietly, like a fish, not to make any noise, and keeping his head out of the water.

When he came out on the other side he found another hollow place, took his clothes off and wrung out the water. He lingered there awhile thinking of the instructions that Sergeant Rough had read to him from a paper the general had given him.

"I remember everything," he assured himself.

He had been walking almost two miles, and he started looking in the distance for some sign of an encampment. He could see nothing but the wide open road to La Angostura.

"Now I shall begin to look for wagon tracks, and feet tracks, on all these hidden paths and roads because Santa Anna knows all about them and his coach must have come by here." With more caution than ever he walked inside the bushes on all fours, searching for paths with broken branches made by wagon wheels. And sure enough, presently he found some coach-wheel tracks, and after them some mule's hoof tracks. This told him the tracks were no less than Santa Anna's coach and his escort behind him.

A tremendous sigh came from his heart. He sat down to recover himself, because the finding had made him—well—just a little agitated, not afraid, not at all; just agitated around the throat and his heart was going pitapat.

"This is *it!*" Pedro said to himself in a whisper, and looked around to make sure of something.

There, to the left, was the very large hollow below the peak of a hill, like a small valley, which Sergeant Rough had told him to look

for. Those Americans knew everything! Pedro
would have wished to find Santa Anna's camp
himself, in another place. But as he walked on
all fours toward the small valley completely hidden by the hill, he could clearly see, under the
bright rays of the moon, a very large tent. He
crawled further down and saw that the tent had
large green, white, and red stripes painted all
over it.

They were the colors of the Mexican flag
painted brightly on the dark tent and under the
moon's rays they looked almost phosphorescent.
Pedro recognized them instantly. He immediately lay flat on the earth and stayed there, with
his ears and eyes alert to the slightest sound or
sign of people around the camp.

Presently, as he heard nothing, keeping his
flat position on the earth, he dragged himself
very cautiously until he was so near to the tent
that he could see the eight-mule coach in front.
For a moment he thought of turning and drag-
ging himself up again and returning to Sergeant
Rough immediately.

"They didn't believe me about the fighting
cocks, and I want to see them and tell Sergeant
Rough I *saw* them." Pedro thought better of
turning back, and feeling a little bolder in the

dead silence around the camp, he stood up and looked all over the place until he found the crates with the birds.

So elated he was that he made too quick a turn and bumped against the broken branch of a tree, making a slight noise. He flattened himself on the ground again and covered himself completely with the poncho, which was the same color as the earth. He heard steps, uncovered one eye and saw a light in the distance, and smelled the tar oil from the torch. But thank Dios no one came. Only the fighting cocks had crowed, awakened by the light. Then silence again. The torch had been put out.

The next morning Pedro awoke in the tent that Sergeant Rough had had set up near to his own quarters, for him and his volunteers. Pedro had slept fitfully and couldn't believe that so much would have happened to him in one day. The crowning glory of his day had been when he had returned safely from La Angostura and had gone straight to Sergeant Rough to report. The sergeant had given him another, much stronger pat on the back, and sent him to bed saying: "Lookout Pedro, you'll hear from the general about this."

He looked around at his volunteers, wondering if he should tell them about his adventure. But they were all asleep, anyway, and perhaps he'd better not say a word. Juan and Guadalupe's empty straw mats were in their corner. "I bet they are awake and doing some work for the Americans," he said to himself.

By now the men asleep were beginning to turn over and wake up. Pedro put his high boots on, with some difficulty, and walked out the tent to look around. He strolled over toward the lookout tower of the Manor House to see if someone was there keeping watch. No one was in sight.

How quiet everything was! And how lonely he felt without his father! Yesterday, Gaspar had taken Don Luis's valuables to the padre, and had not returned. Now that he was all on his own Pedro felt infinitely older than yesterday; and two things pressed hard on his mind, once more.

He thought of Domingo. Why had he not spoken to Sergeant Rough about Domingo? In his grateful heart lingered a great fear that Domingo might be killed by the Americans when they caught Don Luis and Doña Rosa.

"I will tell Sergeant Rough this very day about Domingo saving my life," he promised himself. "And I shall ask permission to send him a message by somebody who might be going near Chapultepec."

A shot from the direction of the lookout tower reached his ears. He looked up and saw several American soldiers in the tower. Then another shot sounded.

"Some signals, some warning!" he thought.

"The battle begins," the men coming out of the tent were telling each other. "What are we to do now, Pedro?" they called to him.

Pedro didn't know what to tell his men, so he pretended not to hear. He walked away, feeling very important in his high boots, with the Winchester rifle he had been given, and with his splendid horse tied to a peg outside his tent.

Sergeant Rough had not given any orders to Pedro's volunteers. Only the young Mexican actually had been made one of them, a soldier with lookout duties.

Not knowing what else to do, Pedro mounted his horse and rode slowly to Sergeant Rough's quarters. He found him standing at the door talking to some soldiers.

"There you are, Lookout Pedro," the sergeant said, but turned away quickly and stepped inside. His square face looked flushed and set, and his eyes very busy looking in all directions.

Pedro thought the sergeant looked different than he had the day before, when he had been so friendly. But all the soldiers seemed to look different, with expressions on their faces of something going to happen any minute.

Another shot shook the air, and Pedro got off his horse and waited at the door of Sergeant Rough's quarters, hoping he would come out again soon. His hands trembled when he held the reins but it wasn't fear that made them tremble. It was the first time Pedro had been in a war and his nerves were on edge. If he only knew what he should do he would feel all right.

One of General Taylor's aides was now trotting toward Rough's quarters. Pedro gave him the proper salute, but the aide had not even looked at him.

Groups of soldiers began to show up here and there in the encampment. When Pedro saw them his nervousness left him and the trembling of his hands stopped immediately. At the sight of the soldiers a tremendous desire for action had taken possession of him.

At last Sergeant Rough came out. "Lookout Pedro, come with me, we're going to see about your volunteers," he commanded.

When they reached Pedro's tent, he said,

"You're going to be part of my rear guard. This means you place yourselves at my rear, facing the other way."

"*¡Viva! ¡Viva!*" Hurray! hurray! All the men, women and children cried to Sergeant Rough's great surprise. He hadn't noticed the women and the children in the camp.

"What are these women and children doing here?" he asked Pedro.

"They are the *soldaderas* and their children, Sir Sergeant. Mexican women always follow their *hombres* to battle with their children," Pedro answered quickly. "They go to cook for them and to cure them when they are wounded, and to bury them when they are killed . . ."

Rough interrupted in a softer tone than was his custom. "But these women and children may get killed."

"They know that, but they wish to die with their husbands, if they have to die," Pedro pleaded. "We love the family more than . . ."

"*¡Basta!* Enough. There's much to do." Rough didn't insist on sending the women and children away, and addressed Pedro. "You settle that, but I want *you* near my headquarters. I might need you."

The midday sun was already scorching the

hacienda. At General Taylor's headquarters the
general, with Wool and other officers, was busy
looking over a map, marking places around the
crosses which showed the Mexican position of
troops, which Taylor and his officers had already found with their field glasses.

"These Mexicans know their terrain and how
to place their men," Taylor remarked. "They
certainly have a large number of them at our
left, between the mountains and the long ravines, on *that* high ground that dominates the
valley." Taylor pointed to the Mexican position
in his map.

General Wool glowered and looked up at the ceiling with that air of doubt he always felt when Taylor spoke. "I don't know if our left is properly defended," he said, looking at Taylor.

"No? What do you know about it?" Taylor snapped and went out with some of the officers to the lookout tower.

From the tower Taylor could see clearly some divisions of Santa Anna's Lancers coming up the Saltillo Road. He could hear their bands playing, but they were still out of cannon-shot range.

Then great clouds of dust blurred the view, and in the field glass danced little figures of Mexican cavalry in their bright uniforms. In the distance the officers looked like puppets in a play, dressed as they were in colored uniforms with bright plumed hats; their flying standards showed clearly against the green trees of the road.

Taylor descended from the tower with a happy face, joking with his officers. He had already given orders to move toward the base of the mountains that bounded that side of the valley. Once again his hunch had proved correct.

Colonel Marshall's regiment was already there, and the Indian Brigade and Gorman's

Second and Third regiments. Other squadrons
would be there soon, dismounted and carrying
their rifles, ready to meet whatever threat there
was to his left.

"Not one shot has been fired yet by Santa
Anna!" Pedro's volunteers told one another,
wondering who was going to shoot first.

They felt proud because of their important
command in the American Army. If Don Luis
could only see them now! While they waited for
Pedro to return from Sergeant Rough's quarters
they proceeded to eat, and after eating to take
their siesta, the midday nap everybody in Mexico takes, war or no war.

And now it was late afternoon. Pedro had returned to his men with a flushed face. "The battle begins soon," he told them in a commanding
voice.

No one said a word, but everybody felt the
very air of the hacienda heavy with echoes of war
noises, though still far away.

At last Pedro, who had been sitting on his
horse giving orders to his men, turned and galloped away from them, shouting, "Not one man
move from here until I return."

He had seen the signal that Sergeant Rough

had told him to watch for by the gate of the Manor House, and rode madly to meet the aide-de-camp, to go with him on a special mission.

A solitary Mexican officer was riding in, dressed in the brilliant uniform of the cavalry, although to Pedro he didn't look like a Mexican.

"I bring a message for General Taylor," the Mexican officer said in English with an Irish accent.

"Follow us," the American aide told the Mexican officer, looking at Pedro out of the corner of his eye. Pedro was terribly disappointed because there had been no need of his Spanish.

"Here is General Taylor, sir," the aide-de-camp said to the Mexican officer when they reached headquarters.

"My name is Patrick Walsh. I am a captain in the Mexican Army. I bring you an important message from General Santa Anna."

The officer handed Taylor a long paper scroll rolled and sealed at one end.

General Taylor took it quickly, peeled off the seal and scanned the writing; his eyes narrowed with anger as he read.

"By all the . . .!" Taylor read parts of it out loud to his officers. "It is dated at Camp Encantada, February 22, 1847, that is today."

You are surrounded by 20,000 men and cannot avoid being cut to pieces with your troops. As you deserve my consideration, and I esteem your valor, I wish to save you from certain defeat, and send you this warning in order that you may surrender at your discretion. You have my assurance that you will be treated with the consideration of the Mexican character . . .

Taylor stopped reading and said with a grin, "He wants to save me from certain defeat! I'll show him the consideration of the American character!" He called for his favorite aide, who always wrote his communications.

"What shall I write, General?" the aide asked.

General Wool spoke up. "One has to be firm, yes, but at the same time polite."

But Taylor didn't listen and was already dictating his answer. He then took the quill from his aide with a deliberate gesture, signed his name carefully, and read his reply to his officers.

Headquarters Army of Occupation near Buena Vista
February 22, 1847

Sir: In reply to your note of this date, summoning me to surrender my forces at discretion, I beg leave to say that I decline acceding to your request,
      Z. TAYLOR,
      Major General United States Army
To
Señor General Antonio López de Santa Anna

It was a wildly happy Pedro who, after escorting the Mexican officer out of the Manor House, galloped back to his volunteers to give them the tremendous news.

CHAPTER 7

Santa Anna Attacks

A<small>T</small> Santa Anna's headquarters great confusion reigned. Officers were kept waiting for definite orders as to when the battle would begin. Santa Anna was keeping to his tent with his favorite, Lieutenant Andrade, but from time to time sending messages to his staff by Andrade.

"Tell them that before night comes the Yanquis shall be thrown into the Rio Grande, like so many sheep," General Santa Anna said, when the answer arrived from General Taylor refusing his request to surrender.

Lieutenant Andrade returned from delivering the message in a very unhappy mood. In spite of his great admiration for Santa Anna and his complete devotion to him, he had not forgotten the terrible march of two hundred miles they had made from San Luis Potosi to Saltillo and at last, to Buena Vista. They had lost thousands of men, some deserting and others dying on the road from hunger, exhaustion and disease.

"We shall attack in one *momentito*"—in a little while, in one moment, he would order the attack, Santa Anna told Andrade, mounting his horse and riding off to inspect his troops.

General Antonio López de Santa Anna was a man of great personal magnetism, and in spite of his fits of temper his soldiers always fell under the spell of his dramatic personality. Before he became "the man on horseback" of Mexico, he lived in retirement on his lovely estate, Manga de Clavo—Spike of Clove—devoting himself to cockfighting.

He was a little over middle height, black hair and eyes, pale, sad face that even his enemies found attractive. He loved personal display, was dishonest and completely ignorant of the realities of life. At times his dark eyes could look like those of an angry mountain cat, and at others like those of a gentle deer. A man of many moods, when Santa Anna was alone he became very calm, almost like a different person. There was a curious side to his nature that he never showed to others. It was the Indian superstitious side, and with him it took the place of religion.

It was in this mood that he descended from his observation post and called to young Andrade, "Go and tell the padres it is time to say Mass for the soldiers." It was his habit to take priests in his army to bless the troops before going into battle.

General Taylor stood on his own observation post, from which he could study Santa Anna's divisions. The Mexican troops seemed to be distributed further to the left than Wool had let him think.

"We're all right, all right," Taylor said to himself. "These Indians have run away from me before, and they shall run again." He went on planning out loud. "The Second Kentucky should be moved out to our right. There's a flanking threat there!" He called to a lieutenant within earshot, "Take this to Colonel McKee. You'll find him half a mile to our rear." He handed the lieutenant the note he had scribbled, sitting on Old Whitey.

Presently, sudden and violent sounds filled

the air. Taylor heard horses' hoofs galloping up
to his observation post. Generals Wool and Bliss
and other officers of his staff were surrounding
him as he sat on his horse with the field glasses
to his eyes. From the distance came bursts of dis-
charges and detonations with repeated and pro-
longed sounds.

Taylor and his officers looked toward the
Mexican lines, spread over the plateau. Santa
Anna had attacked! One of his batteries was
shelling Marshall's men, who were advancing.
But their aim was bad, their shots were missing
the Americans in their frantic haste and poor
range.

To General Taylor, the noise and disturbance
by the Saltillo Road was as yet so much bustle
and hustle. He lit a cigar and continued looking
through the field glass at Marshall's men, now
marching under the thick rows of old trees.

But, presently, stronger detonations came
in repeated succession. General Bliss looked
through his field glass and murmured, "Both
sides are now within range of each other, and
soon they will be engaging with muskets and
rifles." He looked expectantly at Taylor.

General Taylor took the field glass from Bliss.
"I take it there are three to four thousand men

on that hill," he said, scribbling a note and calling for a messenger. "Take this to Major Washington," he commanded, and turning to Bliss: "I've asked him to move his guns toward the hill. Our peg-leg general will try hard to reach the top of that hill." Taylor continued observing the Mexican lines.

"By jiminy!" Taylor exclaimed, suddenly. He had spied a hollow behind the Mexican lines that made him chew hard on his cigar. Santa Anna and his officers in their bright plumed hats were clearly seen in that hollow! He scribbled another note to Major Washington and sent it immediately. This time Taylor didn't say anything to Bliss, not even when in due time, a cannonball from Washington's battery landed precisely on that hollow he had spied.

"A good shot! Look, General," Bliss remarked, handing the field glass to Taylor.

The general took it with a smile. "Sure enough! Santa Anna and his officers! And they are galloping away." He gave a wink at Bliss.

In the next hour or so all the ridges along the Saltillo Road on the Mexican side became invisible because of the great clouds of dust in the air. Santa Anna's Lancers were coming in an endless stream.

"My scouts figured out by the length of their campfires that there must be about fifteen thousand of them," Taylor announced. "Those Lancers are what we have to watch," he warned.

"Can they take our artillery?" Bliss asked, quite sure that they could not.

"We'll see, we'll see," said General Wool with a doubtful glance at Taylor. "Your volunteers might think twice before facing the Lancers." Wool hated volunteers in the army.

The dust on the road cleared after a time and the Mexican military bands were heard playing "Degüello," the cutthroat piece they always play before an attack. The musicians were marching around the circles formed by the Lancers taking positions, their standards now flying in the air. After the Lancers more troops on foot were coming. They were a poor-looking lot of barefooted conscripts, who looked more like ragamuffins than soldiers, but all bravely marching in the direction of the American left.

But "Old Rough and Ready" was not disturbed. He had his left well protected. Colonel Humphry's regiment had dismounted already, and the Arkansas regiment and the Indiana Brigade with the Kentucky cavalry, all were there, defending the left.

Pedro, with his volunteers, protecting Sergeant Rough's rear guard with the zeal of veteran soldiers, had heard that the battle really was on. They were more than eager for action, but they also had heard something else, something that probably the Americans didn't know about. Pedro wished they knew and would be aware.

If a cannonball had landed in the midst of Pedro's little army, the effect would not have been more terrifying. For they had heard the Mexican bands playing "Degüello," and knew what that meant. It meant death to everybody, and no quarter to a living thing on the path of the Mexican Army.

"*¡María Santísima!*—Blessed Mary," cried all the volunteers and the women *soldaderas* in one frightened voice. Complete disorder threatened Pedro's little army.

"What are we?" Pedro shouted. "Are we miserable slaves afraid of Santa Anna or are we soldiers?" He called to them as he rode among his men, trying to calm everybody. "Aren't we fighting for our freedom from the cruel masters?" he cried to them desperately, although he himself was trembling all over and his hands could scarcely hold the reins of his horse.

Constant cannon shots reached their ears.
"Everybody back to their positions," Pedro
commanded in no uncertain tone, and rode
away as far back as he was allowed and found a
high spot from which he could see the battle
front. Thank goodness he had kept Don Luis's
spyglass! He looked through it long. He could
see Major Washington's guns from his two batteries placed in the center of the plateau, and
the gunners rushing madly to their places. Then
a rain of shrapnel began to fall straight on the
slope of the mountain.

The Mexican battery was answering, but hundreds of Mexican soldiers were falling in piles, as they tried to climb up that difficult slope. Pedro couldn't keep his eyes off his first look at a real battle. He scarcely realized what was taking place. The furious attacks and counterattacks from both sides, which seemed to go on forever as the Americans and the Mexicans fought for that hill position, were beyond Pedro's understanding. It seemed to him that the same soldiers in the same places were just killing each other over and over again. "How strange war is!" he told himself, and at last removed the spyglass from his bewildered eyes. He rode back to his position.

The engagement of attacks and counterattacks lasted for several hours of furious fighting without any definite gain to either side, although the Second Indiana regiment, with Colonel Bowles commanding a third gun position, had played havoc with the Mexicans. They had kept bravely coming and dying like sheep, and had at one moment almost reached the crest of the hill. The three American guns concentrated on the top of that hill had saved the moment.

Over the plateau proper the fallen horses and the countless wounded and dead soldiers on

both sides were the silent witnesses of that terrible day of battle. From the American lines the
wounded were being picked up and hurriedly
taken away in wagons to the hospital tents. On
the Mexican side stumbling figures tried to get
up and to walk leaning on their rifles. Some
lucky wounded were carried across the plateau
on the backs of fellow soldiers, only too glad to
get away in the twilight from the terrible American artillery.

Since late afternoon the Mexican batteries
had been moved to better positions, to improve
their range. More troops were coming to try to
outflank the Americans at the left, their muskets
and rifles keeping up a continuous rattle and
flashing of fire.

And night was descending over the battlefield. It started to rain, and the Mexican battery
stopped firing.

"They are coming on quickly," said Taylor.
"Peg-leg is extending his lines. We have to keep
them from that hill. He might try to turn our
flank and we don't want to fall back on Saltillo."
Taylor was silent for some moments, removing
his old cap and wiping the rain off his face with
it. He sensed treachery of some sort, as night was
approaching, and was busy planning. "Bliss," he

called, "send word to Captain Pennington. He is half a mile to our rear. Tell him to have his troops leave their horses and march through the narrow path in line with our left. Tell him I'll be along." Taylor said this knowing well that his men were always cheered and inspired by his presence.

"Do you intend the troops to climb the height?" Wool asked.

"Never mind what I intend," Taylor answered sharply. He was keeping his thoughts to himself and planning the next move. He was thinking that Santa Anna might turn his position during the night. His intuition told him there was something strange about the sudden stopping of the Mexican battery.

Presently the well-known signal gun of the Mexicans, for a respite from firing, boomed three times.

"And that is that," Taylor said. "This is all for the night, gentlemen," he called to his officers as he galloped away.

To Pedro this day of thunder and blood in the distance, with so many soldiers killed without his being able to help in any way, would have been unbearable but for an extraordinary thing that had happened to him just as darkness was falling. He had heard rumbling of wagon wheels on the hard road not far from his station. Promptly he galloped in their direction.

"The dead! The wounded!" Pedro called to his men in a voice full of grief, as he looked in the open wagons with soldiers lying on their backs, covered with blood. Doctors were attending to some, covering others completely, for they were beyond relief. The wagons were on their way to the hospital tents, and a most curious thing happened to Sergeant Rough's rear guard.

It wasn't that Pedro forgot he was in charge of the volunteers and under orders from Sergeant Rough to keep that rear from a surprise attack. But something else happened to Pedro at the sight of the wagons full of wounded American soldiers. And for the moment he forgot everything but those poor *Americanos*.

"Lupe!" he called, and called until he found her. "Where is the hospital where you take the bandages? Where is it? Far?"

"No. I told you to come with me the other day and I would show you where I go, remember?" Lupe answered. "It is just over there, behind that grove of trees." She pointed to the spot.

"Come with me, then." Pedro bent down from his horse, lifted Lupe easily and sat her behind him. "Guadalupe and all the women, follow me, pronto!" he commanded. "All the women to the hospital, at once, to care for the wounded! Bring some lanterns and candles." And to his men he shouted, "Remain here without moving one inch. I return pronto."

"The Americans don't take their women to war, do they?" asked Lupe, as she rode proudly behind Pedro, holding on to his elegant American belt.

"No. Even the nurses are *hombres*," Pedro explained, as if he knew all about the American Army.

"But when soldiers are wounded and dying they remember their mothers and their sweethearts, no?" Lupe asked with a shy look in her eyes.

"Yes," Pedro answered softly, looking at Lupe out of the corner of his eye. "You will make a good wife, I think," he told Lupe in a serious tone, as if he felt himself old enough to take a wife.

Lupe fumbled with her long braids, lowered her eyes and said nothing, for they had arrived at the hospital tent.

"I come to offer my women, the *soldaderas*, who know how to cure the wounded," Pedro announced to the startled doctors, who were looking at the Mexican Indian women with not a little surprise.

"We can use them." The head surgeon, a Texan who spoke Spanish, answered shortly, for he was busy already with his operating knife on a very young soldier who was badly wounded.

Lupe ran to him and stood silent in front of the surgeon, ready to help. Then, as the busy doctor wasn't saying anything, and had not even looked up from his operating table, she spoke, "I am the one who makes the bandages, but I forgot to bring any with me," she lamented.

The surgeon still wasn't paying any attention to Lupe, but presently, when the young soldier was being carried away, he looked at her and seemed impressed by her very clean and neat appearance.

"I tell you what to do," he said, pointing to a pile of blood-stained pieces on a table. "Get the women to wash all that, and to clean up all around the hospital. But don't let them touch my operating table," he warned, with a serious gesture of his index finger. "Do you see that woman there, by the table in the courtyard? I saw her wiping the knives and forks on her *skirt!*"

"*¡En el nombre de Dios!*" exclaimed Lupe, and ran to tell Pedro of the shameful deed before the Americans. But Pedro already had gone back to his position.

When Pedro returned from the hospital tent he found that nothing had happened in his absence.

In no mood to speak to the men, Pedro retired to a solitary spot, dismounted from his horse and made the sign of the cross on his forehead, in memory of the dead soldiers he had seen.

"How quickly, how quietly death comes to soldiers!" Pedro thought.

CHAPTER 8

The Tide Turns

To Pedro, morning came after a sleepless night. In the silence of the hours before sunrise he wondered if everything had been over the night before. Sergeant Rough had sent word to him about the Mexican signal gun that had boomed three times for cease firing, and had asked him to send his volunteers to help to build ditches; but he didn't know if it meant the end of the battle. At the moment, however, there was only silence and darkness over the mountains.

It wasn't long before Pedro saw an occasional

dim ray of light, and heard a shot or two from the outposts of the armies. What could that mean? He sat up on his mat and looked at the volunteers. They had all returned safely from the front, and were still sound asleep. He thought of Lupe in the hospital tent. He felt sure she was awake, too. That would be like Lupe.

Suddenly, awful war noises broke the silence. "The battle is going on for another day!" Pedro said aloud, and awoke his men. He placed them immediately in proper formation, with their backs to Sergeant Rough's rear, to protect it from the surprise attack that he felt sure would come. "Something will happen here today," Pedro told his men.

The American battery at La Angostura had been keeping up a thundering cannonading at Blanco's division, destroying the front ranks of his men. The Mexican troopers were falling in heaps; survivors were making for the roads and hiding in hollows and behind rocks.

Then, from the base of the mountain, Pacheco's battery started throwing shells into the American blue-jacketed line, and his men began to come out of the ravine in droves. It was a disorderly line, but they were spreading

quickly across the ridge, goaded by angry officers with threatening swords.

For hours the American grape and canister
kept sweeping through the Mexican platoons,
which seemed to disappear in the smoke and
dust. Finally, Pacheco's lines broke in disorder
before the constant onslaught of the American
artillery.

The American guns were being moved for-
ward. The entire American left was a thick
mass of blue-jacketed advancing troops, and
mounted men galloping across the plateau.

From the Saltillo Road came only an infre-
quent crash of a gun from the Mexicans. But
from an advantageous height in the mountain-
side, Ampudia's Light Corps still fusilladed the
Americans, who were down on the lower slope,
with deadly fury.

General Taylor was riding across the plateau
followed by his staff, observing the scene. His
unkempt figure on Old Whitey took on an air
of strength and faith that seemed to be felt in
the entire battlefield. He could see Davis advancing to the left, up and up to the hill where
now the Mexican infantry, flanked by the Lancers, were moving. The gun from Bragg's bat-

tery was sending deadly shrapnel. The Mexicans halted their advance, their firing stopped, their front gave way and they fell back on the reserves.

"That's *it!* Good for Davis and his Mississippians!" exclaimed Taylor. "He's making them run away again."

Now only a large force of Mexican Lancers, with fluttering banners, continued to pass at the foot of the hill, trotting toward the Saltillo Road.

"They think they can cut us off from Saltillo," Taylor remarked to his officers.

"Look, General. The Mexican cavalry is re-tiring on their own men."

Suddenly Taylor saw an unexpectedly long line of enemy cavalry and infantry placed along the rear of the plateau. "Their front has shifted," cried Taylor, turning in his saddle to see better the Santa Anna forces, now facing the Saltillo Road. "And we have our back to Sal-tillo!" Taylor murmured under his breath.

"Lieutenant Prescott," he called. "Ride down to Major Washington. Inform him that the enemy is moving down on left to cut the Saltillo Road between his position and Buena Vista. Tell him if he hears firing behind him not to pay attention to it. To hold his position and his guns where he is."

At that moment Taylor saw something that for the first time gave his face a frozen look. The Mexican Lancers, at least fifteen hundred, were riding knee to knee in close column of squadrons down the slope toward the Americans. "This could be the end," Taylor thought.

The Lancers came in a mad gallop, but presently slowed to a walk instead of making a headlong charge. Then, suddenly and unbelievably, they halted.

The Americans opened a devastating fire with muskets and rifles. Sherman's howitzer began to bellow and in an incredibly short time the leading squadrons were annihilated, men and horses going down in heaps. What remained of the Lancers retreated in mad disorder toward the mountains.

"Good enough!" Taylor patted Old Whitey with affection, and promptly gave several orders in a happy mood. Artillery fire was to continue.

He didn't finish speaking. General Wool appeared out of a clear sky.

"General Taylor." Wool saluted very respectfully, this time. "There's a white flag flying near the Mexican heavy battery southwest of the plateau. A Mexican officer brought a message to our advanced line. Santa Anna wants to know what *you* want to do?"

"I want to take his scalp!" Taylor chuckled, but sobered up immediately. "You go over, Wool, and see what Santa Anna is up to. Order the guns to stop firing." Taylor brushed his unruly, thin white hair from his eyes.

It was beginning to rain hard. Taylor, with his staff, rode to a more sheltered observation post, leaving an orderly to wait for Wool's return and bring him to Taylor. It seemed he waited for ages. But at last Wool returned.

With a curious smile on his face, Wool addressed Taylor. "There was no one there," he told him. "Their battery continued to fire, but except for a few volunteers there was no one there, and no one around who knows where Santa Anna is. I can't understand . . ."

Taylor interrupted. "He's fooled us! That was a trick to get what was left of his Lancers off our gunfire."

Wool agreed with Taylor, for once. "I wonder where Peg-leg is? Let's go somewhere else. Nothing can be seen from here."

Taylor was already riding away.

Around Pedro's rear guard only the distant cannonading that had kept thundering all day without letup brought to him and his volunteers the horror of the battle. Nothing had happened near Sergeant Rough's rear guard, until late in the afternoon, when more wagons with wounded soldiers kept passing along the back road. Every time they passed, Pedro rode to meet them and peered anxiously in each wagon, searching for the face of his good *amigo* Sergeant Rough. But he did not find him, blessed be all the saints! He hadn't received a single word from him all day.

Instead, Pedro was surprised to see a large number of Mexican Indian women following the wagons. After them came a long line of ragtag barefooted Mexican soldiers, unarmed. Some were on foot and other on mules. What could this mean?

Pedro rode up to them and asked, "Are you on the side of the Americans?"

They were startled to see a Mexican dressed

in American uniform, but delighted to speak with him. "We are deserters, and we want to go back to Mexico City where we come from," the men walking in front answered.

"Our men are dying like mosquitoes, Sir Colonel," the women called to Pedro respectfully, after noticing his uniform.

"The Yanqui artillery is the very Satan himself," said one veteran soldier in a more intelligent, quiet voice. "Our officers are going *locos*. They say that Santa Anna is not to be found. The soldiers are refusing to obey orders, Sir Colonel," he continued. "We want to return to Mexico City."

Pedro's heart jumped. He spoke to them in a very serious, commanding voice. "Very well. I have many deserters with me. We are *all* going to Mexico City," he told them without knowing how true it was. "Follow me."

At the mention of Mexico City, Pedro thought of Domingo. The Military College was right there, just outside of the city! Could he, should he, when the battle was over, go with these men who knew the way?

He took the deserters to his rear and wondered what to do with the women and their children. He spoke to them: "My soldiers have their women with them, but I have sent them to the hospital to care for the wounded. We are hungry. How many of you want to cook for my men?"

A chorus of voices answered. It seemed that all the women would be glad to cook, and to eat as well, for they were hungry, too. "We have many mules loaded with things to eat, and many bags of corn for the *tortillas* and we have plenty of *cabrito*—young kid—for the barbecues," the women said, "but our men have hidden the mules."

"I know where they left the animals, Sir General." A youngster about ten years old ran to Pedro with the news.

Pedro, who loved kid-barbecue, smacked his lips. "Where are the mules? Far from here?" he asked the child gently.

"I'll show you. They are over there, where the wagons turned," the child answered eagerly. But his mother was pushing him away.

"We'll get the mules for you, Sir Colonel." Several women volunteered to go inside the woods where the mules were hidden.

To say that Pedro was feeling more important than ever at hearing himself called colonel and even general, was to say the least. Of course it was the uniform. The blue soldier's coat did have something embroidered on the sleeve, he knew not what it meant, but there it was.

"We are volunteers fighting with the American Army," Pedro told them later, as he ate his delicious kid-barbecue at mess time. "I am in command of this regiment and everyone of you, now, are under my command," he said, between mouthfuls.

"We brought our trumpets and drums," said some oldish men, timidly. They were musicians and wanted it understood they would rather play for the colonel than fight.

"No drums and no trumpets just now," Pedro commanded. "When the battle is over . . ."

A terrific explosion came from the front lines, interrupting Pedro.

"Just listen to that, in the name of all the saints!" everybody exclaimed.

"And look, Pedro, look yonder at our rear! What is coming!" One of his sentinels, left as lookout, came riding in with the news.

"Sergeant Rough! Sergeant Rough!" Pedro shouted when he saw him riding through his lines.

Sergeant Rough, as he rode along, was looking to the right and the left of his Mexican rear guard in amazement. It was a rear guard the likes of which the American Army had never seen. It looked more like an Indian festival. There was no sign of formation of soldiers. Some were facing front and others squatting and talking and laughing with the deserters. Some were rehearsing tunes in their trumpets and children were running after the butterflies that flew around the fires where their mothers were cooking delicious barbecues.

"Order and silence!" Pedro called, "Here comes our Commander in Chief!" he shouted, when he saw Sergeant Rough riding straight to him.

"Sergeant Rough! What a miracle!" Pedro greeted him.

"Never mind that, Pedro. Listen to me." The sergeant spoke quickly. "We've had a very narrow escape. Those Mexican Lancers are something! There was a moment when they all but broke our lines on our left wing, and tried to cut us off from the Saltillo Road. But the danger is over, that is, for tonight."

"It'll soon be night, Sergeant Rough," Pedro said, looking at the darkening sky. "And, by all the angels, you haven't been killed!"

"No, Pedro. They can't get anywhere near our rear, and you are perfectly safe here."

"I have more volunteers, many deserters . . ."

"Yes, I know." Rough interrupted Pedro with a laugh. "How do you suppose the deserters got through? _I_ let them pass and sent them to you."

"They said nothing to me, nothing," Pedro replied. "But I took them into my army."

"Now listen, Pedro. I have to go back to my post immediately. You keep all these people together. They are going to be very useful. That is, the men *can* help with something we have to do." Rough spoke mysteriously. "As for the women and children, try to see if they won't go to the village, to stay with the good padre."

"Yes, my Sergeant, yes. I will make them go and they will do as I ask them. And can I take them, myself? I might see my father there!" Pedro asked in a trembling voice.

"Yes. You can take them, but be back and keep all your men together and wait here, until I come again, no matter when."

"Shall I take the women and children immediately that you go?" Pedro asked.

"Immediately, and be back at your post. Now I have to leave you . . ."

Pedro interrupted with another, "God bless you and keep you." And Rough galloped away.

Was it a miracle, or was it a dream? Pedro wasn't sure yet. He had just awakened from the first and longest sleep he'd had for ages and scarcely remembered what had happened the day before. Presently, all came back to him. He remembered that night had come, and the fighting had stopped completely. And he had fallen asleep so soundly that at the moment, although the sun was blazing, he hadn't the slightest idea what time it was. But he knew that it must be very late.

He looked at his men. They were still asleep and snoring loudly. Could the battle be over? If he could only ride up front to Sergeant Rough! But he remembered he had commanded him to wait where he was and to keep his men together; and that's what he would do. But if he could only go up to the hospital and see what Lupe was doing, and what they knew there! But he couldn't do it. He must *not* leave his men one single moment.

The thought of Lupe made Pedro think of the long talk he had had with his father and with the padre, when he took the deserting women and children to the village.

"We like the Americans, for they are good people," the padre had said. "But we are Mexicans and love our country. You, Pedro, will grow up to be a benediction to Mexico and the poor workers. You must learn to read and to write and become a leader of men in our poor Mexico. I shall find a good tutor for you, as we have no schools."

Pedro had replied that there was nothing in his heart he would like to do more than to learn to read and to write. But first he must stay with Sergeant Rough and obey his orders.

"If that is his duty, now, Pedro must do his duty," Old Gaspar had said to the padre. And then to Pedro, "But you, my son, after the battle is over, if God spares you and Sergeant Rough, then you must do what the padre tells you to do."

As Pedro thought over everything that the padre and his father had said to him, his mind was greatly troubled. At one moment he was for staying, forever, with Sergeant Rough; at the next he felt sure that he loved his father and Mexico more than anything in the world.

"And I wonder about the good Lupe!" Pedro had spoken frankly about her to his father, as Mexican young people do to their parents. And his father had said:

"It is well. Your mother was fifteen when we married, and you have grown into an *hombre* already."

That had settled many things on Pedro's mind. When the battle was over and he had finished his duties to Sergeant Rough, he would build his own very beautiful hut somewhere away from the hacienda, and marry Lupe.

But he thought of Domingo and Mexico City

again, with renewed anxiety to go to the young master. Before anything else he must get to Chapultepec and look for Domingo at his Military College. He must explain to him everything he had done and *why* he had gone to the side of the Americans.

But there was Sergeant Rough! Riding with him was General Taylor, and with him other officers of his staff.

Pedro stood at attention, speechless, until Sergeant Rough came to him and gave him one of his strong pats on the back.

"Come with me for a ride." Rough brought his horse on a line with Pedro's. "I'll show you something, Pedro."

They rode to Santa Anna's headquarters. The place was abandoned. All through the woods and the roads they met barefooted Indian soldiers in bloodstained rags. Some were squatting silently and others were flat on their backs, moaning. From the distance came the rumbling of wagons, the voices of men calling for wounded men to pick up, women weeping and children screaming.

"Those poor people!" Sergeant Rough exclaimed. "Santa Anna got away during the night and left his soldiers to shift for themselves.

There are thousands of them walking and dying on the Saltillo Road, back to goodness only knows where. But we are not taking prisoners."

"I know they all fought bravely. We Mexicans have valor, my Sergeant, and love our land." Pedro pleaded for his countrymen.

"Yes. I know, Pedro, and I'll tell you something. Your people fought so well that when the fighting stopped in the night even General Taylor had no idea that Santa Anna would retreat."

"I don't understand . . ."

"I mean, Pedro, that our artillery was killing your brave Mexicans by the hundreds, and still they kept fighting until night came. General Taylor expected Santa Anna to continue his attack this morning, and we were all surprised to find that your Mexican general had escaped during the night."

"Then the war is over!" Pedro exclaimed with glowing eyes.

"No. Not the war. But we are through with Buena Vista, and General Taylor is very happy. He has sent a communication already to President Polk announcing victory. You see, Pedro, Taylor is now master of all the north of Mexico and the general expects to become the President of the United States after all his victories."

"Oh! He will not fight us any more? The general will go back to the United States right away?" Pedro asked, not understanding much of what Rough was explaining.

"Yes. I think so, Pedro. But now I am taking my men to Mexico City and I am taking *you* and some of your men with me . . ."

Pedro interrupted with a tremendous sigh, and he did something soldiers don't do. He grabbed the sergeant's hand and kissed it humbly, with tears in his eyes, as he would kiss the padre's hand in church. "Miracle of miracles!" Pedro kept repeating. "I shall soon see Master Domingo!" He went on mumbling under his breath as he took the large, white handkerchief that Rough was handing him to wipe his tears.

"Now, come, Pedro. Soldiers don't cry," Sergeant Rough said.

So Pedro patted his horse and followed the great *amigo* Rough in a mad gallop back to the hacienda.

CHAPTER 9
Pedro's Great Dilemma

BACK at the hacienda Pedro felt bewildered. There were things going on he did not understand, but he dared not question anyone. Many days had come and gone, and not a word had been said about starting for Mexico City. At General Taylor's headquarters there was great rejoicing and the officers had settled down as if they were going to live in the Manor House forever.

"Even the soldiers are celebrating and settling down also, as if they are going to stay," Pedro said to himself.

His only clear thought was that Sergeant Rough had said they were going to Mexico City. But when were they going? Was he ever to get to Domingo in Chapultepec!

Pedro didn't know that General Taylor was constantly sending and receiving and waiting for runner-messengers with important communications from various places. He had expected the general and his troops to march away immediately, back to their United States.

He was confused and grief-stricken. His constant thinking, without speaking to anybody about it, made Pedro almost ill; but nothing surprised him more than when Sergeant Rough said he was taking him to his doctor at headquarters. For a moment his lips moved silently, then he said definitely, "I am not a sick one, my Sergeant."

"No, I know, Pedro, but we are going on a long journey and Doc is going to look me over, and I want him to see you, too," the Sergeant insisted.

Rough had had a confidential talk with the doctor about Pedro. "I have a Mexican lad I am taking with me, and I want you to look him over."

"Okay, send him in," the doctor had agreed.

"As you will see he is tall and strong but I think he is younger than what he says he is. I want to know if he is physically fit for the long journey to Mexico City."

"What seems to be the matter with him?" the doctor asked.

"He weeps now and then, and that is not like him. Pedro is one of the bravest youths I have ever met, knows no danger, but I think he has gone through more than he can stand."

"Are there any more symptoms you have noticed?"

"No. Only the weeping and it always comes when someone is kind to him. I think it is his way of showing he is grateful."

"I've noticed that about the Mexican peons," the doctor remarked. "They are not used to kindness and when something nice happens to them, they always cry. Funny, isn't it?"

"You look very good to me, only a little tired," the doctor told Pedro after he examined him.

"I told the good sergeant that I wasn't sick, now you can see I am *not*." Pedro said, very pleased and relieved not to have to have any more cold instruments put against his body.

Pedro lost no time in returning to Sergeant

Rough with the good news. He found a number
of the deserters with him. These men who had
deserted Santa Anna, and Pedro had taken into
his army, had been selected by Rough to go with
him to Mexico City because they came from
there and knew the roads.

"They must be making plans for us to start
on our journey," Pedro told himself.

"Come in and tell me what you have been
doing," Rough called to Pedro.

Before Pedro had time to reply, Rough announced, quickly, "I have good news for you.
Do you remember that General Taylor promised to send a message to your *amigo* Domingo,
in Chapultepec?"

"Oh, yes, yes. Did he?"

"Yes. And there is an answer for you. Listen!
I'll read the answer to you." Rough took a note
out of his pocket and read it: " 'Domingo
Ramos Blancos, son of Don Luis and Doña
Rosa, of Buena Vista, is at the Military College
in Chapultepec. He has received the message
from Pedro, son of Gaspar, the overseer of the
hacienda. He wants Pedro to go to Puebla immediately, where Domingo's mother is alone,
because Don Luis, his father, died during the
journey.' "

"Don Luis is dead!" Pedro exclaimed between his teeth. "But I want to go to Chapultepec, to see Domingo. I do *not* wish to see Doña Rosa, at all, not at all . . ." Pedro's cheeks flamed with anger. "Only Domingo I want to see," he begged anxiously.

"Now, Pedro, we'll talk about this later. I'm very busy now. I tell you what you should do. Go to stay with your father and the padre until I send for you. Now go."

"Yes, yes. I do so want to give my father all the news."

Rough walked with him to the door for a last consoling word. "The general will tell us more about the trip to Mexico City soon, now good-by."

"Master Domingo is well, at his college in Chapultepec." Pedro said the moment he saw his father squatting at the door of the padre's house.

"My son, my son! I hardly know my son!" Old Gaspar exclaimed, looking at Pedro in his American boots and uniform he now wore constantly. "Come with me before you see the padre. I have something to tell you, dear son of my life!" The father led him to the back where he was living in a little house which the padre had given to him.

"Lupe, Lupe. Come to see who is here."

With Lupe came Pinto, who went wild at seeing Pedro.

"Who found Pinto?" Pedro asked without explaining. He had lost his dog but hadn't mentioned it because he had forgotten where he had left him, in all the tremendous confusion at the hacienda.

"I brought him with me, my son, when I came to stay with the padre," Old Gaspar answered.

"Pedro loves Pinto more than anything. Don't you, Pedro?" Lupe asked when she saw Pedro embracing, and even kissing Pinto's ears.

"I was just thinking that we must have a partridge hunt and surprise Sergeant Rough with a big, big bunch of the birds."

"Yes. But first tell us everything that is happening at the hacienda," pleaded Lupe, sitting at Pedro's feet, admiring his elegant soldier's uniform, and brushing Pinto away.

"I have so much to tell," Pedro said. "First, Don Luis is dead."

"Then may he rest in peace," Old Gaspar said, calmly.

"And what do you think?" Pedro continued.

"Doña Rosa is in Puebla, alone." He didn't know if he should mention the letter from Domingo to him.

"How do you know all this?" his father asked.

"Sergeant Rough knows everything. He told me."

"The padre knows everything, too, but he didn't tell me about Don Luis. Have you been told about Santa Anna? Only yesterday another of Padre's runner-messengers came to tell him how the one-legged general was marching through all the towns, in his eight-mule coach

with his fighting cocks, proclaiming victory over the Americans."

"No. I haven't been told that."

"And he has two American standards waving from his coach, that Santa Anna says he captured," his father continued.

"Victory over the Americans!" Pedro repeated. "He ran away . . ."

By the seventh of March, General Taylor's plans were complete. He was master of all the north of Mexico. He went back to Saltillo and placed his army on the offensive. The next move would be on Nuevo Leon, the adjoining state.

"A very important step," Taylor told himself. He knew he would do better following his hunch than if he obeyed orders from Washington.

He had been asked for more reinforcements for General Winfield Scott, and hadn't minded sending a small detachment of his troops.

"We'll see what 'Old Fuss and Feathers' does round Mexico City," Taylor thought, calling Scott by his nickname. And it was just as well to let Sergeant Rough go with his men as part of the reinforcement. Rough would keep him posted on what Scott was doing.

And, at last, with Sergeant Rough's command went Pedro! Pedro, and the selected Mexican deserters from Santa Anna's army were on their way to the capital.

Santa Anna, in the meantime, had arrived in Mexico City, proclaiming victory over the Americans. A revolt of students, called Polkos, was going on. Santa Anna promptly put it down. He was acclaimed by the populace as the man of the hour, and immediately assumed the presidency of Mexico. Then, more sure of himself than he had ever been, in spite of his constant defeats by the United States Army, he set about opposing the Americans.

He managed to confiscate church property and private property and collected millions to set up the new army. He knew that General Winfield Scott was coming from Veracruz, after his victories around the port. He selected the pass of Cerro Gordo, near Jalapa, the capital of Veracruz, to stop the American advance.

Santa Anna considered his position at Cerro Gordo impregnable, and established strong fortifications, but a terrific bombardment by the American artillery turned Santa Anna's position on a flank, and on April 17, he fled to Orizaba. General Scott had all but destroyed the Mexican

troops of about twelve thousand men at Cerro
Gordo and was ready to march on to Mexico
City through Puebla.

"To Puebla!" Pedro exclaimed when Sergeant Rough told him they were finally on their
way to the very city where Domingo had asked
him to go, to stay with his mother.

"Yes, Pedro. It is strange we should go to
Puebla," Rough remarked. "You see, there
wasn't any need of us at Cerro Gordo."

"Then, we're not going to Puebla just to—
eh—to leave *me* there with Doña Rosa?" Pedro
asked, half in fun and half in earnest. After all
the strange things that had happened to him,
nothing could surprise him any more.

"You don't think we are running the war for
Doña Rosa, do you?" Rough laughed. "And
after Puebla, Pedro, we will be in Mexico City
in no time, and *you* can go to Chapultepec to
see Domingo."

Pedro only smiled. He seemed to have gotten
over much of his emotion. But never in his life
would he forget this endless caravan of American military wagons, stopping at times to pick
up a tired or sick soldier that had fallen out of
the lines. All this had a very definite impression
on Pedro's thinking.

"War is a sad and terrible thing," he told himself. "I wonder how Domingo feels about this war?" Pedro dared not speculate on how Domingo felt about *him* joining the Americans! As yet, he hadn't killed a single soul! God had not permitted it, although he had been ready to kill even Santa Anna if need be.

He was thinking of all that had happened at the hacienda, when all he had wanted to do was to be free and to help the workers to free themselves from Don Luis. He must talk all this over with Domingo. Now that Don Luis was dead, Domingo was the master and the heir to all Buena Vista.

"So now, we are going to Puebla to join General Winfield Scott who will take us to Mexico City," Pedro grumbled to himself, impatient at the delay to get to Chapultepec. "And Doña Rosa is in Puebla." He grinned knowingly. "If she tries to keep me from going to see Domingo, I shall run away, from her and from Sergeant Rough and from the entire American Army." His cheeks grew hot as he planned secretly to run away from Puebla without further delay.

CHAPTER 10

Pedro Goes to Chapultepec

GENERAL Winfield Scott with his army was already in Puebla when Sergeant Rough and Pedro arrived. The general had marched into the lovely city, Puebla of the Angels, several weeks before, on May 15. He had been received with open arms by the clergy, who was all powerful, and acclaimed by the entire populace.

Everybody knew of Santa Anna's defeat at Cerro Gordo, and the Bishop of Puebla had made a proclamation to the people: "If we have to choose between the Americans and Santa

Anna, better we have the Americans," the Bishop had told them.

There had been no resistance to the American troops, and General Scott was being entertained royally, while waiting for further orders from Washington. Old, aristocratic families opened their homes to the *simpático*—charming —American general. They had been impressed by his courteous personality, and the precise and orderly entry into their beautiful city.

Although General Scott was in his sixties and in not the best of health, he appeared robust and seemed to be enjoying very much the splendid meals in the homes where fiestas were given daily in his honor.

Santa Anna had preceded General Scott by four days. He had come to Puebla at the head of two thousand cavalrymen, riding straight to the governor's palace, knocking down men, women and children, with deliberate intent to frighten everybody. In spite of his threats to the authorities, and demands from the clergy to raise money for the defense of Mexico against the invaders, every move from the Mexican general was ineffective.

He had prepared a written proclamation to the people of Puebla, giving them his instructions of what to do when the Americans came to take over the city. When he read it in the public square the few people there did not pay much attention. For four days the desperate general loudly insulted the local authorities, in public. His cavalrymen terrified the peaceful inhabitants in the outskirts. But Santa Anna got nowhere, and many of his men were deserting him.

On the fourth day, Santa Anna decided to force his way into the governor's palace, which had been denied to him. Stumping stolidly on his brightly painted black peg leg, he walked through the streets toward the governor's palace to insist on seeing the governor, who had refused to give him an audience. But that was the very day when General Winfield Scott was marching in with infantry, squadrons of cavalry, and many batteries. Santa Anna saw the people laugh with joy, watched everybody coming out of their houses, where they had been hiding; and saw the clergy, all about, smiling and welcoming the Americans. And before anyone knew it, Santa Anna and his troops disappeared.

It was late in the afternoon the day Pedro arrived in Puebla. Sergeant Rough was not reporting at General Scott's headquarters until the following day. He wanted his men to rest after the long journey, and Pedro had been quartered for the night with the soldiers in the barracks of Scott's army.

"From Puebla to the capital is only about thirty or forty leagues," Pedro said aloud. He was planning his escape to Mexico City, while pretending to be asleep in the barracks. "The Military College is in the Castle of Chapultepec, right at the entrance to the city. I will find it immediately," he told himself, feeling dreadfully lonely. "Should I ask permission of Sergeant Rough? Should I see Doña Rosa? Domingo will ask me if I saw his mother in Puebla, and what can I tell him?" Never had Pedro been so puzzled as to what he should do, and he tried to sleep. But he couldn't.

"I could leave now and find the roads before the night gets very dark." Pedro, wide awake, was reconsidering his plan of action. But at the sight of the countless soldiers sleeping in the large barracks, he feared that some of them might still be awake. Deciding to wait until he was sure that all were asleep, he covered himself completely with the blanket he had found on the cot that was his bed, and came to a definite decision. Not until then did he begin dressing himself under the blanket.

"Poor Domingo," he whispered to himself. "I shall go immediately to find his mother."

The padre had told Pedro that Doña Rosa was staying in the Bishop's house, under his protection. Now that he felt sure that all the soldiers were asleep, he walked out of the barracks in his white cotton peon pants and shirt with his poncho over the shoulder. Nothing would have made Pedro happier than to have Doña Rosa see him dressed in the elegant uniform of an American soldier, but he felt safer in his peon clothes.

He had no idea where the Bishop's house was but his intuition told him it must be near to the Church of The Rosary. The padre had mentioned that church as the most wonderful in the world, with altars of pure gold. He had asked him to go and say a prayer in that church. Surely the Bishop must live right near there.

He walked through the deserted narrow streets and saw through the low balconies of the houses candles and lamps burning inside. "The whole world is awake, afraid of the Americans." Pedro shook his head. "If they knew them as I do, they wouldn't be afraid."

At last he arrived at the main square, walked

under the arcades, and presently saw a magnificent church that he knew must be The Rosary. He felt like going in to say the prayer the padre had asked him to say, and perhaps to find a priest who might give him the Bishop's address. He tried the door. It was locked. Instantly he heard a shot coming from the back of the church.

¡María Madre de Dios!—Mary Mother of God! Pedro hastened to hide behind an enormous old tree by the side of the church. A priest came out from one side and another from another; both armed with rifles and calling: "Who goes there?"

Pedro came out of hiding, shouting at the top of his voice, "A servant with a message for Doña Rosa of Buena Vista, Good Padres!"

The priests looked Pedro over carefully. One of them asked, "Where is the message?"

"In my head, as I know not how to read. But here is something that Domingo, the son of Doña Rosa wrote that I should do." Pedro took out of his trouser pocket Domingo's written message that he always carried with him, and handed it to the priest.

"Domingo Ramos Blancos!" the priest repeated after reading the message. "We know very well the son of Doña Rosa." Both priests spoke, smiling at Pedro.

"Come with me, son." One of the priests led Pedro to the side door and took him into the sacristy.

The other priest remained on guard outside in the back of the church.

"*Muchacho,* you might have been shot!" the good-natured priest warned Pedro. "We are guardians of the treasure in this church. Don't you know that Santa Anna has ordered all the gold treasure in the churches looted and melted?" the priest asked without expecting an answer. He was busy putting on a long black cassock, and handing to Pedro a garment that acolytes wear. "Put it over your clothes. I'm taking you to the Bishop's house."

Of the many disguises that Pedro might have imagined, this one was the most wonderful. He walked by the side of the priest wondering if the padre would have let him wear it if he knew that he had turned against Doña Rosa.

What Doña Rosa herself thought of her old overseer's son standing in front of her wearing an acolyte's garment with natural grace, his handsome dark eyes serene and his head held high, Pedro never knew.

"I come to tell you, Señora, of a message that Domingo sent me," Pedro said without pretense to be anything but what he felt himself to be—a free young man.

"From *Master* Domingo." Doña Rosa corrected Pedro, taking the paper that he had placed on a table by her side.

She did not look at Pedro, for it was one of her habits not to look her servants in the face. After reading Domingo's request for Pedro to stay with her, she spoke in a plaintive tone. "My dear, poor son! He knows I am sad and lonely, but Domingo refuses to leave his Military College and come to me." Doña Rosa broke into uncontrollable tears, to the great surprise of Pedro. Was this his old mistress talking to him!

Pedro's heart responded to the mother's grief. "Señora, I'm going to see your son, and if you wish I can take him a letter from you . . ."

"*You* are going to Chapultepec, to see Domingo? Did he send for you? I know he is fond of you. He told me about the man hunt . . ."

"Domingo saved my life," Pedro interrupted, "and now, Señora, I am going to save his life. If the Americans *have* to fight in Chapultepec and he can't get away from his Military College in time . . ."

"Pedro, Pedro! I never thought that *you*, an ignorant peon, could have such noble ideas. God

has heard my prayers," Doña Rosa said, without explaining.

"I don't understand you, Señora. But I must hasten. My journey is a secret one and I must get out of Puebla tonight," Pedro whispered, standing up. "If you wish, I will take Domingo a letter from you."

"You don't have to make a secret of your journey to see my son. The Bishop will give you all necessary papers to make the trip safe for you all the way." She started to pull at a cord to summon a servant.

"No, no, no, Señora." He stopped her. "No one must know. I'm running away from—eh—from someone, I can't tell you." Pedro bit his lips angrily and started for the door.

"I know everything, Pedro. The padre at Buena Vista has told me everything that has happened at the hacienda. You are sorry now, that you went to the side of the Americans, no?"

"No, no and no!" Pedro exclaimed from the heart. "The best *amigo* I have is an American sergeant."

"Poor, poor misguided *muchacho!*" Doña Rosa exclaimed. "But I forgive you, Pedro."

Doña Rosa's patronizing tone infuriated Pedro. He wanted to say many things, but he must go now, he must get away from her. "I have to go, Señora. I don't have to have any papers from the Bishop. I know I can find my way."

"It is sixty miles from Puebla to the capital, Pedro. They say Santa Anna has troops on all the roads, all the way. You will probably be killed before you reach Chapultepec," she pleaded. "I know that if the Bishop knows you are going to help Domingo to escape from his College, the Bishop will send you in one of his carriages all the way to the Military College . . ."

"In the carriage of *Nuestro Amo*—Our Lord?" Pedro asked piously. He knew that all Mexico revered the carriage of *Nuestro Amo,* in which the Bishops and the clergy in general rode around the streets in times of trouble and distress.

"Yes, Pedro. The Bishop must know that you are going to see Domingo. He is now his guardian and the executor of our estate." Doña Rosa finished with a sigh of relief.

Pedro opened his eyes very wide and thought it over for some minutes. To ride in one of the carriages of *Nuestro Amo* was indeed a great blessing. "If you wish for me to speak with the Bishop, I will."

Pedro sat inside the carriage of *Nuestro Amo*, next to a priest, dressed in the red and white ritual garment of the acolyte. The black-robed priest held the gold chalice covered with an embroidered cloth.

"My own mother wouldn't recognize me if she saw me," Pedro was thinking as the carriage moved quickly along the roads and very slowly, when they passed villages and cities. In the cities the black curtains over the carriage windows were drawn aside, for the people to see the gold

chalice that represents Our Lord on earth. People, when they saw it, knelt on the streets as the well-known carriage drove slowly along. Soldiers and civilians recognized the insignia of the Bishop of Puebla, and respected it. Puebla at that time was not only the center of Catholic power but the most important military stronghold in the entire country; and long before that moment insurrection had broken out between clergy and the Mexican Government.

Slowly, peacefully, the Bishop's carriage rode

through town after town, for many days, stopping in the cities for a restful night at the local Bishop's house. At last they reached the suburbs of Mexico City: Contreras, Churubusco, Molino del Rey and Chapultepec!

"There is the castle, Pedro. We have arrived." The priest pointed to the Castle of Chapultepec high on its hill where the Military College was situated.

Pedro couldn't say a word for some moments. He had never seen anything so magnificent and he felt very shy. "The College door is where, Good Padre?" he asked presently. He could see many, many doors to the castle and he knew he would have difficulty there.

The priest ordered the carriage to drive to the door and left Pedro there, after speaking to a sentinel on guard. "I shall wait for you and Domingo in the forest." He pointed to the grove on the right side of the castle. "Take this letter from the Bishop and this one from Doña Rosa and give them to Domingo." The priest stopped to extract a leather pouch from under his black cassock. "Give this to Domingo, when *no one* sees you. Now God be with you."

Even before Pedro climbed the second, long winding stairway of the Military College, on his

way to Cadet Domingo Ramos Blancos' room,
he knew that an escape from the College would
be impossible.

"One more flight, and turn to the right," a
servant who was showing Pedro the way called
as he was about to turn back downstairs. "Ask
for Cadet Ramos Blancos of anyone you meet."

Pedro climbed up one more flight but saw no
one to ask, and felt perplexed. He wondered if
he should not hide somewhere, just hide without speaking to anybody, until Domingo came
along and surprise him. His simple Indian way of
thinking didn't work in the more complex ways
of a big city. No sooner had he thought of hiding, than a group of five cadets came out of one
of the rooms on Domingo's floor, where Pedro
was now standing. They didn't even stop to look
at him. They took him for one of the *mozos*—
servants—in the College and were walking downstairs, when Pedro ran after them.

"I bring a letter to Señor Domingo Ramos
Blancos," he called in a subdued voice, which
nevertheless echoed loudly along the gallery of
the old castle.

"In there you will find him." One of the
cadets pointed to the very room they had just
left. "That *muchacho* looks from the country-

side. I hope he doesn't bring *another* letter from his mother. Poor Domingo!" The cadet sighed, with narrow, angry eyes.

"Walk in, walk in." A feeble, sickly voice that Pedro didn't recognize for the moment answered his knock.

On a very elegant white bed, his head on a very large white pillow, Pedro's startled eyes saw the figure of a young man, pale and thin.

"Pedro, Pedro! It isn't possible! How did you

get here, *muchacho?*" Domingo suddenly had
come to life. He sat up and pulled at Pedro's
hand and made him sit very near his bed. "But it
seems impossible, to see you here." Domingo
was surprised but plainly overjoyed.

"Are you sick, Master Domingo? You have
grown thin and pale."

"It is this war, Pedro. And my father's death,
and my mother who will not understand what I
want to do." Domingo confided in his young
servant as if he were his most intimate friend.

Pedro's heart was melting with heavenly joy,
but he only bent his head and said, "I bring you
a letter from Doña Rosa and one from the
Bishop of Puebla and . . ." Pedro looked around
to the door he had left open, to see if anyone
were spying outside, before giving him the
leather pouch.

Sure enough, a man in uniform was standing
by the door. Pedro turned to Domingo and
whispered. "And I have something else for you,
but someone is listening."

"Godfather, Godfather, walk in. You'll never
believe it. Here is Pedro from the hacienda. I've
told you about Pedro whom I left deceived,
waiting for me, and I never went back." Domingo was relieved to say this before Pedro.

General Nicolás Bravo walked in slowly, dignified in his uniform. Domingo's godfather was the commandant of the College and of the garrison at Chapultepec. A distinguished old soldier, he belonged to a very different type of military men from the upstart Santa Anna. General Bravo had fought nobly in the battles for independence, and was training his cadets to be worthy officers in the Mexican Army, when there would be no more Santa Annas.

While Domingo read his letters, General Bravo had a long talk with the young country lad who seemed to him a very unusual youth, for his station in life. Pedro felt at home with Domingo's godfather, and opened his heart to him without hesitation. He told him everything, except about Sergeant Rough. About that, Pedro intended doing something alone, in secret, perhaps escaping back to Puebla just to explain everything to his good *amigo* Rough, and then get right back to Domingo.

Domingo had finished reading his letters and had written two short answers, one to the Bishop and a longer one to his mother. "I've written, for the last time, what I feel I must do," he said, looking at his godfather. "To my mother I have repeated what you know I have written many times before, and to the Reverend Bishop I have said just what you have advised me to say." Domingo smiled at both Pedro and his godfather and said, suddenly, "Now I feel hungry, Godfather. For the first time in days I feel hungry!"

"This is the first day in a long time that I see Domingo looking and feeling like his old self!" The general looked at Pedro when he spoke, as if to say that his godchild had been helped by the reunion with him.

Pedro, not knowing what he should say or do now that the answers to the letters were ready for him to take back, stood up and waited silently for orders.

"Where did you say the Bishop's carriage is waiting?" the general asked Pedro.

"From here I can't show you, but I will show you when we are outside."

"No, Godfather. Don't let Pedro go back to the carriage. I know how he is, and they may make him . . ." Domingo stopped to look at the glowing face of Pedro. "I want Pedro to stay with me as my personal *mozo*."

"Do you hear what your master wants?" asked the general.

"God bless him, sir," answered Pedro, unable to say another word.

"Then *we* shall find the Bishop's carriage." With a very happy face the godfather pulled at a cord to summon someone. When a young subaltern answered the general's bell, he met him at the door, gave him a note he had scribbled, and Domingo's letters. "Give this to your captain and return to report." The general looked fatherly at Domingo and at Pedro, and on second thought, he called the subaltern back. "I shall be in my office." He had decided to leave the two young people alone to enjoy their reunion. "And you won't have to worry about anything any more, Pedro. You're staying in the capital. Look after your master."

CHAPTER 11

The Battle of Chapultepec

CHAPULTEPEC CASTLE, seat of the Military College, was an important fortress for the defense of the City of Mexico. At the time of Pedro's reunion with his young master, Domingo, the war with the United States was expected to end at any time. General Winfield Scott had remained in Puebla and there were rumors that Santa Anna had ordered a cessation of fighting and was negotiating peace with President Polk of the United States.

Pedro's devoted care of Domingo helped the distressed cadet to recover his health and spirits.

157

They passed pleasant days horseback riding and talking about the hacienda.

The friendship of master and servant grew daily. One afternoon Domingo returned from his classes unusually happy. "I've been talking with Godfather about you and Old Gaspar. I told him that I want you to be my overseer at the hacienda and your father the manager."

"You are our master, now!" Pedro exclaimed. "Will you stay in Buena Vista all the time?"

"Not all the time. I must continue my studies and not disappoint Godfather. Our country needs many good and intelligent officers in the army."

"But during vacations you will come and . . ."

"And we will hunt and we will ride and we will swim, and I shall see if you can read and write well by that time." Domingo had started teaching Pedro how to read and write.

Days pass quickly when two young people are happy in each other's company, but it wasn't long before a great cloud fell like a sudden storm over Chapultepec, and over Domingo and Pedro.

"The negotiations at General Scott's headquarters in Puebla have failed," Domingo's godfather announced one day late in August. "The President of the United States sent a Mr. Nicholas B. Trist to bring about a settlement with Santa Anna, but everything is over." General Bravo shook his head sadly.

"But the invasion of our country will be stopped, no?" Domingo asked.

"There are rumors that Santa Anna is selling our country to the United States, while pretending to set up fortifications along the outskirts of the city. Of course, that traitor could cut communications all the way to Puebla if he wanted to," he said, clinching his teeth.

"Our soldiers are eager for battle, all over Mexico," Domingo remarked. "It is Santa Anna that kills their fighting spirit."

"Yes, my dear Domingo. Santa Anna has been putting up defenses for years, and then falling back under attack, abandoning men and artillery. The man is insane!" The general showed Domingo, on a map, the places where Santa Anna had withdrawn his battalions when he should have advanced.

"Why can't you make *me* a lieutenant-cadet now, dear Godfather? Please let me lead some troops . . ." Domingo was afire with patriotic zeal.

"Because I want you here. I need you for the future of Mexico. And your mother needs you.

She is all alone now, and you're very young. Besides, the Americans will be stopped, yet!" The general gave Domingo a warm embrace. "You stay with me. We'll fight them here, if they reach Chapultepec."

"Yes, yes! You should hear our little group planning what we would do if we were older, or even now, if you would let us . . ." Domingo belonged to a group of five cadets—the ones that Pedro had seen coming out of his room the day he arrived—and these boys were the pride of the College for their studies and patriotism. His godfather knew whom Domingo meant by the little group when he interrupted him.

"You and your fellow cadets will shame your elders yet, and be remembered forever in the history of our country." General Bravo had dedicated his life to the training of worthy officers at the Military College, and was very proud of this particular little group of cadets only seventeen years old, and with more sense than many of their elders.

One day Pedro came with extraordinary news.

"Today I rode to the Old Peñón, the hill you told me was seven miles from the city, right near the road to Puebla," Pedro told Domingo. "Do you know what I saw?"

"What did you see? You look as if you had seen a ghost."

"Gun emplacements, many, many, everywhere, and white tents in a very large encampment . . ."

In less than a week the City of Mexico was completely fortified against the American invaders. And Santa Anna's proclamation to the people had been a startling warning:

"When you hear our cannons in Chapultepec boom, it'll mean that Scott's army has started to march from Puebla for our City of Mexico."

A few days later, the great sixteen-pounder cannons boomed from Chapultepec early one morning. The Military College had been expecting it. General Bravo's garrison had been prepared for any attack. Frantic fathers of many of the cadets had demanded that their sons be evacuated and many of them had been removed.

Domingo and his little group, with a dozen or more other youths, whose fathers were enemies of Santa Anna and great admirers of General Bravo, begged to remain. General Nicolás Bravo, their commandant, proved himself the true soldier. To him these brave boys, who some day would be the real officers in a happier Mexico, should experience war and know what war really was. The general agreed that the boys who wished to remain should do so.

Domingo was happier than he had been for a long time. He was eager for action, along with his little group. So one day he was surprised to find Pedro in his room, packing all of Domingo's books, clothes, the pictures from the wall, his uniforms and other personal belongings. "What on earth are you doing?"

"Everything is ready. I must do what I promised your mother," Pedro announced simply, although he had never mentioned helping Domingo to escape from the Military College.

"Who ever told you *I* want to escape, little *loco!* I am a soldier and intend to fight for my country. Now, you unpack everything at once," Domingo commanded.

General Bravo was coming into the room. Pedro left, with a respectful bow, but very perplexed. Was it possible that Domingo was staying in the College! He knew that the castle was the first place the Americans would attack, being the fortress at the very entrance of the city. What was he to do now? All he could do was to stay very near to Domingo, every minute, and save him if possible.

"I've just returned from seeing Santa Anna. I asked for more soldiers for our garrison." General Bravo spoke standing before Domingo, looking every inch the soldier that Domingo dreamed of being himself, someday. "Where is your little group?"

"In their rooms. They are all ready and eager to fight, dear Godfather."

"Now, listen carefully, Domingo." General Bravo took a map of the castle from his pocket and showed him two rooms in one of the towers, high above, looking down on the hill where the castle was built. "In these two rooms I want you and your group to stay, if and when Chapultepec is finally stormed." He made some crosses in the places. "Now, go and get the boys and see if you can find the rooms. Take the map with you and when you return wait in your room until I come."

When General Bravo finally came into Domingo's room, he had had an argument with Santa Anna, he said, who had threatened to dismiss him. However, Santa Anna had changed his mind.

"We found the rooms," Domingo told him.

"I knew you would." The general looked about him. "Where is Pedro?"

"As usual, squatting outside the door," Domingo answered, and called him.

"Pedro, from now on I don't want you to leave the College. You stay at all times with your master and be ready to bring me his messages," General Bravo commanded. "Now, I want you boys to move your things to the rooms in the tower. Pedro will bring your meals. You are not to leave those rooms without my permission." The general stood up to go.

"But Godfather, I thought we were to take part in the fighting. There are no firearms in the rooms."

"There will be arms there. I shall send what is necessary, when it is necessary."

Pedro remembered the last words of General Bravo the rest of his life. His keen Indian intuition told him that the time had come. He felt that Domingo was in terrible danger, and he was ready to prove his great love for him, who had saved his life, but what should he do?

The Americans were coming nearer, nearer. Messages from Domingo's godfather came often with news, and with reassurances, but Domingo and his little group were not reassured. They wanted to know exactly where the American forces were and be in the fight.

"Why are we kept in the tower, like chickens in a coop?" Domingo was losing his patience.

"Because your godfather knows what he's doing," answered the Leader, his more sober thoughts telling him that it was best he didn't mention to Domingo what he had heard when he sneaked down to the dormitory of the College, during the night, to talk with his fellow cadets, who knew everything that was going on.

He had heard that Santa Anna was trying to have the Mexican Congress accept a dictated peace, without success. That the American General Winfield Scott was advancing from Puebla into the Valley of Mexico. That Santa Anna had turned the City of Mexico into a battlefield for a defensive campaign. That his favorite Generals Mora and Robles and Cano had been placed in command, and the generals in turn were robbing haciendas and emptying jails and conscripting entire villages of men, who were already arriving daily in the capital.

"How can I tell Domingo all this?" The Leader felt sure he couldn't mention it to his sick fellow cadet.

Santa Anna had selected the Old Peñón hill, which Pedro had reported seeing full of encampments. Conscripts were digging trenches all around the hill and inundating the meadows. Exactly thirteen thousand trees had been cut to build trenches and barricades.

Prouder than ever, Santa Anna one day rode out of *El Peñón* at the head of several of his regiments, stopping here and there to proclaim to the people greeting him from the roofs, that there was nothing to fear from the Yanquis.

But Santa Anna's fast runners kept bringing the news of the American advance to his headquarters. Some reported that the Americans had arrived at San Martín. Others that they had stopped at Río Frío. And, at last, that the Yanquis were on the ten-thousand-feet-above-the-sea-level rocky summits.

"From that height the Yanquis can have a good look at our Valley of Mexico," Santa Anna told his officers. "That's about all they are going to have, a good look."

"Let them come down, if they can. Wait until they see our Old Peñón!" exclaimed General Valencia, who was to defend the town of San Angel, near the capital, with his fifty-five hundred picked troops.

But the Americans were coming down from the rocky summit, slowly but surely. Their guns, batteries and wagons with baggage were descending, pulled by an orderly stream of horses, wonderful to watch.

And on the eleventh of August, the American vanguards were at San Isidro.

Santa Anna, back in Mexico City, continued to feel sure of himself, in spite of the American advance. The entire populace had forgotten differences of opinion. Everybody was united and up in arms, literally, against the invaders.

At last a report came that the Americans were advancing toward Old Peñón, as Santa Anna had suspected. But another report announced the Yanqui army in Mexicaltzingo, after taking the village with tremendous loss to the defenders. And yet another report contradicted that and said the Americans were at Chimalpa or at Tulancingo. No one knew exactly where Scott's army was marching, and at Santa Anna's headquarters there was nothing but confusion.

"In the name of all evil, where are the Yanquis?" Santa Anna was having scouts and runners punished for their stupid mistakes.

But at last it dawned upon Santa Anna and his staff that Winfield Scott had tricked them.

General Scott had made a feint advance on Old Peñón, then had marched his army through a neglected mud-choked road that Santa Anna thought to be inundated by the recent rains. On this road, around the lakes of Chalco and Xochimilco, Scott had marched his troops and moved his supply wagons and heavy guns twenty-five miles in a day and a half, along the all but washed out and forgotten route.

By the eighteenth of August, Scott's entire army was camped in San Agustín, ten miles to the south of Mexico City, a town the general knew to be on the unfortified side of the capital.

Santa Anna immediately ordered the transfer of the troops from Old Peñón to the new front that Scott had initiated. The populace, finding themselves unprotected, turned against Santa Anna.

"What difference does it make *where* we fight the Yanquis?" Nonchalantly, Santa Anna boasted to his staff, pretending indifference to Scott's movements, but he went on erecting defenses in the undefended south.

By the nineteenth, Santa Anna had fortified every town on the way to the capital, and General Valencia was ready to defend the most important hill in San Angel, with his five-gun battery.

That very afternoon Winfield Scott attacked San Angel. A desperate battle went on all day, with heavy fighting for the key hill position, the Americans repelling the furious Mexican counterattacks with their superior artillery and battalion-size forces. When night came and Scott's gunfire had stopped, they had outflanked General Valencia and isolated him on the hill.

Santa Anna was camped with the Pérez brigade of eight hundred cavalry and some artillery, three-quarters of a mile behind the Americans, and was planning to send reinforcements.

At six o'clock the following morning the Americans struck front and rear and Valencia was lost. His picked Lancers deserted him and the infantry was thrown into disorder. Foot soldiers and *soldaderas,* mules, artillery, horses, all fled in a grand descent from the hill.

"It took us exactly seventeen minutes," Commander Persifar Smith was telling his men, as he looked at his watch. "Let's see what we have here," he added, looking over the booty. "Two guns, *our* guns!" he exclaimed, pointing to the American guns that Santa Anna had captured at Angostura.

By noon Santa Anna's reinforcements arrived. A desperate afternoon of fighting followed. Attack after attack was driven off by the Americans, but killed and wounded on both sides were estimated in the hundreds. Finally the Mexican attacks broke off toward the early evening.

By sunset the Americans were again on the march, advancing toward Churubusco, which they took easily. Then on to other suburban towns of the capital on the path of the American Army until at last Scott's troops occupied the entire defenses around Mexico City.

Santa Anna, back in Mexico City, was sitting in his office in the National Palace with his officers. "We've lost about five thousand killed and more than twenty-five hundred prisoners, with eight, *eight* of my generals!" He spoke gently, with a catch in his throat, in the manner he sometimes used to get sympathy. "Also, we have lost many cannons and a vast quantity of ammunition." This time he forgot his gentle mood, and pounded on the floor with his peg leg, his face twitching with the pain that came from the flesh against the wood.

"Take this to General Scott, personally," Santa Anna ordered Mora, after he had written a proposal to the American commander for a truce.

General Scott accepted and proposed a short armistice. But two long weeks dragged on with negotiations with Washington, for a possible peace. The United States demanded New Mexico and Lower California, with the Rio Grande as the southern and western boundary of Texas. They also offered a cash settlement. The Mexicans would not hear of it. Their beloved country to be given away, just like that! Better to be completely destroyed!

But Santa Anna, who had not lost his crafty ways, sent back a counterproposal to President Polk. He demanded a larger sum of money and made other demands, too extravagant to be accepted.

The armistice came to an end. Santa Anna and his officers, in the National Palace, were looking over a map. "Scott will try to take Chapultepec," he told them. "I have everything planned for its defense. Listen to me carefully." He spoke in an encouraging tone, when he saw that the officers' faces didn't look too eager. "The brigades of León and Rangel will be placed at El Molino del Rey, where Pérez is already garrisoned at hacienda Casa Mata. We'll have four guns there, with two divisions of Lancers under Torrejón. Understand?" He wiped his face with a perfumed silk handkerchief.

The officers stammered something under their breath. General Mora spoke out, "The defense appears to be very good."

"Magnificent!" exclaimed Santa Anna. "And I want all the guns on Chapultepec to be made ready at once." He stood up and became rough again. With a motion of his hand he waved the officers, and even Mora, out of his office. "You know very well that Scott, with his tired eight thousand Yanquis can *not* break through all that!" he called boastfully after them, as the officers descended the marble steps.

It was the morning of September the twelfth. Domingo and his fellow cadets were awakened before sunrise by terrific gunfire. Pedro came running into the room, and they all ran out to the parapet, each with his field glasses. They could see from this highest tower in Chapultepec Castle, the City of Mexico in the distance. The balconies and the roofs of the houses were full of people. Faint echoes of shouting reached their ears. Bands in the distance played martial music. And below, in the courtyards of the Military College, soldiers from General Bravo's garrison were coming and going in endless lines.

Domingo and his little group looked at one another without speaking, their ears still tingling from the sudden cannonading that had awakened them. They ran back to their rooms, took the revolvers that General Bravo had sent, and fastened on the leather belts. At the last moment Domingo decided not to put on his belt, and handed it to Pedro. "You put it on, and carry my revolver until I need it."

Pedro was overwhelmed with joy. Wasn't that what he needed more than anything else? When the time came, he would kill anybody who came near Domingo!

Toward evening the boys had decided to send

Pedro with a message to Domingo's godfather, as the Military College was already being hit directly. But daybreak came, and Pedro had not returned.

They had stayed outside their rooms all night, standing on the high parapets, keeping their thoughts to themselves. Only Domingo, now and then, heaved a big sigh and deplored having sent Pedro out. Later he told the boys: "Perhaps it is just as well I sent him. Godfather might need Pedro. He is such a clever and useful *muchacho*."

The Americans had kept their batteries going and now shots and shells were falling right over the summit of Chapultepec. The boys could see grape, canister and shells fall over the trees of the forest, where one part of General Bravo's garrison was stationed. They watched their soldiers answering the enemy shot by shot and screamed with joy when they realized their garrison still was there, defending their College.

It wasn't long before they could no longer see anything clearly, for the smoke and the confused movement of soldiers everywhere, and the changing of the positions of guns, and many things the boys could no longer make out.

The American infantry had moved nearer the

fortress of Chapultepec. The boys realized this was the critical moment. "If they take the fortress, Chapultepec is lost!" The Leader of the little group spoke calmly.

"Then we shall fight! Fight like true patriots and show our elders that we, the cadets of Chapultepec, are not like the riffraff of Santa Anna," Domingo told them, slowly, putting his hand to his feverish forehead. He felt very, very sick, and a headache had been torturing him all night.

His favorite friend came to him. "Come into your room. I want to give you your medicine, now that Pedro is not here."

Domingo followed his friend, silently, to his room and closed the balcony doors against the noise and distress below and all over Chapultepec now.

Out on the parapet again, the boys with their field glasses, looked at the balconies on the floors below. Every balcony and window sill and parapet in the castle was full of soldiers, shooting back at distant American targets. Suddenly all Chapultepec seemed to be a curtain of flame. Domingo looked around for his friends but they had gone back to their rooms, and he went to his, quickly, and sat down to write a letter to his god-

father. There was something he wanted him to
do for Pedro, in case anything happened to him.
The letter ended with: "Don't forget I promised that good *muchacho* that he would be the
overseer of the hacienda and his father the
manager . . ."

A tremendous noise right under his balcony
made Domingo stop writing. For a moment all
his faculties seemed paralyzed. He stepped out

onto the parapet and heard Pedro's voice far
down below, then found him with his field
glasses and called to him.

Pedro looked up and saw Domingo on the
parapet. "Master Domingo, they won't let me in
the castle," he was shouting at the top of his
lungs, frantically motioning up to him with his
sombrero, drawing his attention to an enormous
ladder that had been placed against the castle
wall. Pedro was trying to climb it to reach
Domingo.

"What on earth is Pedro doing?" Domingo said to himself. But at that moment he saw an American soldier was pushing Pedro out of his way, and he had fallen to the ground. "Poor Pedro!" he exclaimed. "But what are these ladders?" Domingo asked himself aloud. He didn't remember seeing any ladders against the castle the last time he had looked out.

Soon he knew. They were American ladders for their soldiers to climb inside through the balconies below. In turn, the balconies of the castle were full of Mexican soldiers. They were thrusting the ladders away as fast as they were put up, with the Americans tumbling down. Domingo saw some of his fellow cadets, who had remained in their classes, out on the balconies, helping to thrust the ladders off the walls.

The sight of the American soldiers climbing up the ladders was more than Domingo could bear. Something told the patriotic cadet that very soon the fortress of Chapultepec would be taken completely by the Americans. Domingo hurried in to his secluded tower room. For endless minutes he walked up and down, up and down and wondered where his little group was. Strange he hadn't seen any of the boys for some time!

He ran to their room. The door was locked. He called and called and knocked at the door frantically. But there was no answer. He broke the door down savagely. The young cadets were on the floor, their pistols near each one. They had shot themselves! Domingo fell over their bodies in a torrent of tears. He touched them and embraced them and felt their limp hands tenderly. Finally, with dry eyes, he ran out of the room.

Calmly now, he remembered seeing a large Mexican flag flying from a pole at a small window of the tower. He went straight to it and pulled it down with a feeling of exultation and great love for his country. Carrying the flag, he walked downstairs to see what had happened inside the College. The floors where the cadets once lived were completely abandoned. Inside the rooms he saw several of his fellow cadets sprawled here and there on the floor, all dead. He hurried up again, back to his room, and walked up and down in a haze, trying to think clearly.

"Poor, dear Godfather! How well he knew I would be protected up here," he spoke to himself in a strange, hoarse voice. "If he only knew what I am thinking!" He went to his desk and wrote a few more lines on the letter to his god-father, and ended it with words of such deep affection for him, and for his mother, that tears flowed in a stream down his cheeks. Then he wrapped the Mexican flag around his cadet uniform and put on his blue cap.

Without further hesitation he stepped out on the parapet outside the room where his dear little group was dead and stood there for some moments as if to say to them, "I am here, right outside your room. I didn't forget you."

At that moment Domingo heard Pedro's voice calling him from below, but nearer to him. He looked down and saw him. This time Pedro was actually climbing up on one of the ladders that reached the floor below him; climbing up in front of an American soldier! What could this mean?

Pedro had been looking up at the parapet every minute, watching Domingo, and had placed the ladder right below where his master stood. He could see Domingo's face clearly and the Mexican flag he had wrapped around his body. Pedro called to him, frantically, "Master Domingo! We are coming to get you. The war is over. American soldier is *amigo*. He is helping *me* to come to get you . . ."

Domingo heard Pedro as in a dream. He saw the American soldier climbing up with Pedro with blurred eyes, but his sight cleared for Pedro. He looked at him for a long moment, called his name several times and waved to him.

But Pedro had no time to answer Domingo's wave. His horrified and unbelieving eyes saw Domingo deliberately walk to the very edge of the parapet, wrap the Mexican flag tighter around his body, then look down at the precipice below for a quick moment and throw himself off crying at the top of his voice: "*¡Viva México!* Long live Mexico!"

Pedro would have fallen off the ladder but for the American soldier who held him. The soldier was also horrified to see the young cadet die so heroically for his country. And, as he was a young soldier, a tear rolled down his cheek.

"Are you all right?" the soldier asked Pedro, who was weeping desperately and trying to get down that ladder as quickly as he could. "Don't push me or we'll both fall," the soldier said, holding fast to Pedro's arm.

"That is my master, my dear, dear Master Domingo!" Pedro screamed. "I must go to him. Why didn't I stay with him every minute, as his godfather told me . . ." He struggled desperately in the American soldier's arms.

Pedro was very ill, for weeks, after Domingo's tragic death, and when he was well again he went back to Buena Vista, where General Bravo saw to it that the last wishes of his beloved godchild, Domingo, were immediately carried out.